Lover, adventurer, and psychic, now Ford's
ready for the assignment of his life ...

T5-DHA-406

FRANCO

ASHES TO ASHES

I saw her as clearly as if she had been dipped in luminous paint

It was Karen's ethereal companion and the expression on that tormented face was clearly pleading with me for something.

The apparition turned, showing itself in clear three-dimensional profile. It gazed down upon the patio, back to me, then once again onto the patio, as though summoning my attention to something there.

I did not give it a second thought nor a moment's hesitation but moved quickly to the balcony. The apparition had winked out with my first step forward but I could still sense presence out there.

That particular presence, however, was not now the focus of my attention.

The focus was immediately below. Two men stood at the patio bar in twilight, a woman in an evening dress was walking toward the pool—and in the pool, submerged in deep water, a nude female figure floated face down.

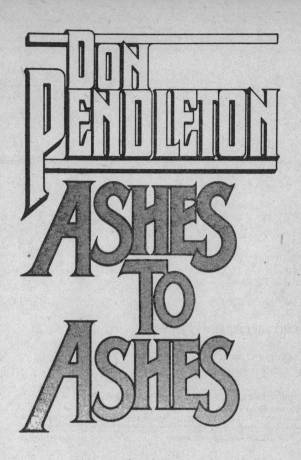

DON PENDLETON

ASHES TO ASHES

POPULAR LIBRARY

An Imprint of Warner Books, Inc.

A Warner Communications Company

POPULAR LIBRARY EDITION

Copyright © 1986 by Don Pendleton
All rights reserved.

Popular Library® is a registered trademark of
Warner Books, Inc.

Cover art by Franco Accanero

Popular Library books are published by
Warner Books, Inc.
666 Fifth Avenue
New York, N.Y. 10103

 A Warner Communications Company

Printed in the United States of America
First Printing: April, 1986

10 9 8 7 6 5 4 3 2 1

Dedicated to the memory of Gustaf Stromberg, late Mount Wilson astronomer and Carnegie astrophysicist, whose fine mind and incisive writings have revealed more than the world is ready to understand about our realities.

"Earth to earth, ashes to ashes, dust to dust; in sure and certain hope of the resurrection unto eternal life."

—Burial of the Dead,
   The Book of Common Prayer

"This analysis of our knowledge of the universe has given us reasons to believe that, behind the world of phenomena we perceive with our sense organs, there is another world to which we can not apply our ordinary concepts of space and time."

—Gustaf Stromberg,
   The Soul of the Universe

Case File: Surrogate One

Prefacing Remarks...

This was my first "surrogate" case. I would regret taking it on almost from the first moment, and I would resolve many times during the progress (or descent) of this case never again to work this particular type of problem. But, hell, she seemed so damned scared—so vulnerable—so, uh—okay, say it, so damned lovable.

My sacred, cardinal, Number One Rule: Never become emotionally involved with a client.

My unfailing, unremitting, forever Number One Problem: It seems that I am always in violation of Number One Rule.

The truth, of course, is that I am in the wrong line of work. I should have been an actor, or maybe a model. I could probably get away with those Marlboro man–type ads. A stuntman, maybe, except that

I really do not take any particular delight in flinging my life recklessly toward the closing jaws of death.

I am almost a lawyer, but not quite—almost a psychologist, but I got bored with a term paper. Could have been a cop, I guess, but discovered in time that the pay and benefits are about equal to that of a garbage collector—and, when you think about it, the work is about the same. Not that both jobs are not vital to a civilized society. I'd just rather someone else handle the trash work.

I was actually trained to be a spy, courtesy of the United States Navy. Naturally they did not call it that. But, hell, a spy is a spy by whatever tag or acronym. Not cut out for that, either.

Maybe I wasn't cut out for anything in particular. I think I would like to conduct the Boston Pops. I have never been invited to do so. I would give it a shot, though, if they would give me time for a crash course in music theory.

This is all very dumb, isn't it? I know what I'm cut out for, why I'm doing what I do for a living—and, to tell the truth, I could not conceive of ever doing anything else. I love my work, with all its built-in problems and uncertainties. I am where I need to be, doing what I need to do. I even enjoyed this case. Well . . . most of it.

For the record, I am Ashton Ford. American born and educated. No connection to the automobile family. The "Ford" was, I guess, a result of Mother's weird sense of humor. Seems that I was conceived on the backseat of a car. She was a South Carolina Ashton, from a family with roots in the American

Revolution. I was born when she was thirty, living independently and comfortably on a nice trust from her grandmother, amoral. I use that last word in the kindest sense possible. Mother was a hell of a lady. Free thinker, that's all. Never married, never wanted to. Never told me who my father is, and I never asked. Just thankful that the name on my birth certificate is not Volkswagen or Oldsmobile.

Great-grandfather Ashton was a naval hero of sorts. I was raised in naval academies, went on to Annapolis and several war colleges, ended up in Strategic Studies—the "Star Wars" stuff—got out as quick as my obligation would allow.

That's enough background for now. It's enough to know, at this point, that I am where I need to be, doing what I need to do—emotionally involved with troubled ladies. I call this a "surrogate" case because that is exactly how it began. I was hired as a sexual surrogate by a beautiful nonorgasmic woman who was just damned sick and tired of dry runs. As usual, the stated problem was but a symptom of a far deeper problem. And this beautiful, lovable, vulnerable young woman had a hell of a problem that no amount of loving would help.

I neglected to reveal that I am a sometimes-psychic. Some have called me a "mystic," but I would not go that far. What I am, I guess, actually, is a lover. So how did a nice guy like me get mixed up in a case like this? That is exactly what I am about to tell you. Turn the page.

CHAPTER ONE
And Death Smiled

He looked about two-eighty of solid beef and had a lot of mean energy in the eyes. Kind of guy you'd rather give a sweet smile and wish a nice day or else disregard entirely. From where I stood at the moment, I had neither option. He was coming at me with apparent felonious intent, moving swiftly along my side of the net like a linebacker sniffing blood. Mine. I had one of those inane thoughts—Wrong game, guy—but I didn't voice it, nor did I consider it prudent to inquire as to the name of it. I learned a few games ago that he who gets there first with the most is usually the one who walks away smiling. So I let the ball sail on past me to meet the gorilla instead, with my best backhand, the tennis racket angled edgewise and moving toward maximum effect.

He grunted and went slowly to his knees, mean energy dissolving instantly into sick passivity and maybe a bit of bewilderment. I wanted to say, "Oops, sorry, wrong ball," but I decided it was no time for humor. Besides, a gorgeous redhead had run onto the court, and I had the impression that she was mad as hell with me—maybe because she called me a dumb shit.

So I went to the net and thanked the flustered tennis pro, then went to the sideline for a towel while the irate lady fussed over the stricken giant. I put the towel around my neck, casually lit a cigarette, and headed for the locker room. The redhead intercepted me about halfway there, fire in the eye and ready to storm all over me. I tried to disarm her with my patented boyish grin but it didn't work.

"You did that on purpose!" she cried. And, yeah, furious.

I didn't try to deny it. I just said "Yep," and kept moving.

"You're an animal!" she yelled after me.

That was my first meeting with Karen Highland. And Bruno. That was a Wednesday. I didn't see them again until Friday, early afternoon, Malibu. This time they came to my office—or to what passes for an office. Bruno held the door for the lady, then came on in behind her and very quietly took a chair at the back wall without once looking me in the eye. I figured, okay, now we understand each other. She was in an easier frame of mind, too, though obviously quite nervous.

I stood up and offered her my hand. She took it, murmured her name, gave me an appraising look as I gave the appropriate reply, then dropped my hand and took herself to the window. Nice view from that window. Pacific Ocean surf, Santa Monica skyline curving into the distance, lots of blue sky. I had the feeling she was seeing none of it.

I was really struck by her beauty. The hair about shoulder length and lying in a soft up-flip, sort of piled a bit at the top and falling into waves at the forehead; velvet cream skin that invited contact; wide-spaced oval eyes of a shade I can only compare with wild violets—but fear there, yeah, fear or desperation or maybe both. She had the long, clean lines you see on showgirls, draped very fashionably in a simple cotton dress that somehow nevertheless managed to look very expensive.

I was struck, yeah—which is probably why I blew this meeting too. I tend to be a bit defensive when I respond this way to a prospective client.

"Let's try this again," she said softly from the window. I had her in profile, feet planted wide apart, hands clasped behind her, shoulders sort of tight, lovely head tilted downward.

I had one of my flashes at that moment. I'll tell you more about those later. For now just believe me when I say that I did not see Karen Highland in that flash; what I saw was another person, older—sick, maybe, or otherwise burdened to the breaking point with some terrible problem, very frightened and very much in need of help.

It flashed on me, then dissolved before I could really inspect the apparition. I shot a look toward Bruno. He was staring at the ceiling. I had been thinking about it since she called me that Wednesday night for the appointment, and I'd decided to tell Miss Highland that I had too many things going right now, and would she call me again next month or next year if she couldn't find another counselor.

All that changed in that flash. I went to the window and put my hands on her shoulders from behind in a light massage—she was carrying a lot of tension there—and suggested that she make herself comfortable.

She had told me, that night on the phone, "Bruno is mute. He was just trying to attract your attention."

And I had told her that he looked like a head-hunter to me, that he invaded my tennis game, that I'd felt it only prudent to sit him down before inquiring as to his intentions.

"He was flustered," she explained. "We'd been trying to catch your attention for several minutes. He's just very direct. And you wouldn't look toward us."

I could have explained to her, but did not, that my concentration on a game of tennis approaches that achieved by a Zen master, so I could buy her apology.

"Does he read lips?" I asked her, present time, with a glance at Bruno as I escorted her to a chair.

"He's not deaf," she replied, "—just mute."

"Then he is not going to sit here during this consultation," I said flatly.

"Wait in the car, Bruno, please," she said without hesitation and without raising her voice.

The big guy was up and out of there almost before she finished speaking, as though he had received those orders before they came in there and he was just awaiting his cue.

I let the door close behind him before I retreated to my desk—well, it's sort of a desk—more of a table with a couple of small drawers, really—acrylic, transparent. Serves the purpose without getting stuffy.

There was a long, almost tense silence while the lady and I exchanged smiles. Finally I asked her, "So how can I help you, Karen?"

She dropped those amazing eyes, brushed nervously at her lap with scarlet-tipped fingers, waited a moment as though trying to construct a sentence, then replied, "I was referred to you by someone at Zodiac."

Zodiac is a metaphysical retreat up the coast near Santa Barbara. I kept on smiling and said, "Someone?"

"I don't know her name. Well, I—actually—I wasn't actually referred. I just overheard this conversation." She swept me with those great eyes. "And I figured—maybe—you're the one."

"The one for what?"

"To—to help me."

"To help you do what?"

She was staring at her lap again. It was like pulling teeth, opening this one up. I told her, "I'm not a medical doctor, you know."

"Don't need one," she murmured.

"Nor a shrink."

She showed me a small smile. "Well, maybe I do need one of those. But that's not what—that is not why I am here. They said you're into all this stuff."

"All what stuff?"

"The stuff they do up there. And that you'd written this paper about—well, on uh, against asceticism."

"I did do one of those," I agreed, remembering, and remembering also the furor at Zodiac over that paper. It was actually a treatise on cosmic sex and the way it really ought to be, the way it could be if people's heads were on straight. The people at Zodiac—or a good number of them, it seemed—were trying to leave the carnal plane behind without dying first—some, without living first. I thought it was bullshit and I said so in the paper.

"I read it," she said quietly.

It was my turn for the lap-inspection bit. After several seconds of high-voltage silence I lifted a direct gaze her way and said, "And . . . ?"

"I'd like to try that."

"You'd like to try that what?"

"What you said in the paper."

I'm sure my smile was a bit forced as I replied to that. "Okay. Why not? Can't hurt you, I guess, with the right guy. But I would not recommend Bruno."

That amused her. "I inherited Bruno when my parents died. He's like an uncle. No, uh—I was thinking of you."

I already knew that—but was hoping like hell, still, that she would not say it.

I told the beautiful lady, with all the professional aplomb I could muster, "Doesn't work that way. I don't work that way. Fall in love. Try it on your honeymoon."

That seemed to sting her. A nostril flared. I could

feel the self-consciousness oozing away. When she spoke it was gone entirely. "Three cheers for old-fashioned morality." Stung, yeah. "You disappoint me, Ashton."

I was rather disappointed in myself, to tell the truth. But I did not tell her that truth. What I did tell her was, "I am not a professional anything, you know. I have . . . certain insights. People have found me out. Sometimes I . . . agree to help them with specific problems. But I do not rent myself out for sex. There's a name for that. I'm not it. But what is your real problem?"

"What?"

"Why are you really here?"

"I told you."

"Bullshit."

"What?"

"Bullshit. I saw her, when you were at the window." I described the apparition. "Anyone you know?"

She had become very pale and her hands were shaking as she struggled with a cigarette. "Then you're really for real," she said quietly, giving up on the cigarette.

I did not respond to that.

After another long moment of silence the lady said, "I've seen her too. It's spooky. I . . . I think, maybe . . ."

I lit the cigarette for her—one for myself too—gave her another moment to get it back together, then prodded. "You were thinking, maybe . . ."

"I don't know, it sounds crazy, I never talk to

anyone about this. I have been seeing her since I was a little girl. Not—I don't mean—not all the time, nothing like that. But ... now and then ... special times."

"Such as?"

"Oh, if I'm sick, or upset about something or ... well, and since I've grown up she seems to appear more frequently and now she's ..."

"What?"

"I think she's trying to communicate."

"How does this manifest?"

"What?"

"In what way does she attempt communication?"

"Nothing ... physical. I just get this ... awful feeling that she's trying to tell me something."

"Something important."

"Yes. It seems very important. But then she ... wisps away."

"Wisps?"

"Like smoke dispersing."

I said, "Uh huh. Who is she, Karen?"

The reply was whispered. "I don't know."

"No idea at all?"

"None." This reinforced with a decisive shake of the head. "But I think she ... wanted me to ... to find you."

"Why do you think that?"

"I just do. Don't ask me to explain something I don't understand myself." A bit of fire again. "She wanted me to."

I mulled it for a moment, then: "What exactly do

you want from me? No bullshit. What do you want?"

"Maybe I want two things."

"By the numbers, then. One?"

She took a deep breath. "One, help me get rid of her. No, that's number two."

I supplied the necessary prompt without blinking an eye. "And one?"

"Teach me cosmic sex," unblinkingly came right back.

"Because?"

"Because I just might kill myself if you don't."

"It's that bad?"

"Believe me, it's that bad." The fire was back, full blaze. "Look, to hell with pride. I have tried everything there is to try. I am not a frigid woman, believe me, I'm not. I am very responsive, highly responsive. To a point."

I did not have to feign sympathy. One of the awareness kicks I had tried involved a process of sexual arousal right to the cresting point and then backing off, over and over. I tried it for about a month. I developed a stammer, could think of absolutely nothing but sex, and had a hard-on all the time.

So I did not have to feign sympathy, no. "One point below bliss, eh?"

"Always one point below."

"Nonorgasmic."

Getting edgy again, almost hostile: "That's the dirty word."

"Since when?"

"Since forever."

"What does your ethereal companion have to do with it?"

"Oh shit!" She was on her feet, moving toward the door. "I knew you'd get to that! Forget it, huh? Just forget it!"

"Sit down!" I commanded loudly.

From the door: "Go to hell!" Out, then back in again, furious: "This must have been a great treat to your ego! Well, forget it! Temporary insanity! Do you think I have to pay a man to fuck me?"

She was gone before I could have replied to that, if I'd had a mind to, which I didn't. I'd handled it very badly. I knew that. And I was already formulating a plan to telephone her as soon as she'd had a chance to cool down.

But I did not have to do that.

She was back again within seconds, standing in my doorway all pale and shaking. "Help me," she moaned. "Something is wrong with Bruno."

But I could not help her all that much. A lot was wrong with Bruno. All was wrong with Bruno.

He was seated behind the wheel of a shiny new Mercedes, not a mark on the body, but also no pulse and no heartbeat. There was no response whatever to twenty minutes of CPR. The paramedics took over and tried for another ten minutes or so, then they simply covered him and transported him to wherever lifeless bodies are taken.

"Did you see her?" Karen asked me in a stricken voice as the ambulance rounded the corner onto Coast Highway.

Yeah, I saw her. She'd moved into the ambulance behind Bruno and was staring at us through the rear window as it pulled away from the house.

And I am certain that she was smiling.

CHAPTER TWO
Ashes

Let me assure you very quickly that I am not into spiritism, black magic, nor the occult arts. It offends my sense of universal order to even admit the possibility that some sort of dark forces could be consciously manipulating this reality of ours. Ghosts, banshees, and demonic spirits simply do not represent my concept of an orderly universe.

So I have an automatic resistance any time I am confronted with phenomena of this nature. I have been confronted, yes, time and again. But I have always sought a nonphenomenal explanation to account for them. Sometimes I have succeeded in that, sometimes not. But I do not let the failures deter me.

I am very much aware, you see, that we inhabit a phenomenal universe—phenomenal, that is, from the ordinary viewpoint allowed by the usual human sense perception. Atomic theory itself is an occult, highly mysterious, and largely incomprehensible concept even to those who are schooled in it. To say to me that the table in front of me is a solid object capable of supporting my weight with ease, but then to go on to explain that, of couse, it is more of an empty space than anything else—other than that, an electromagnetic field more than anything else—that it is the relativity of my state of being in relation to the table's state of being that allows me to perceive the table (and myself) as a solid object, well, say, what could be more phenomenal than that?

Is the table a solid object or is it not? The answer is yes and no. Remove all the space that separates the quarks and widgets and other esoteric elementary particles that go to make an atom, then remove the spaces that separate the atoms—shred the molecules, in other words, and throw out all the space—and what is left is enough matter to maybe fit the hollow of your palm, except you could not hold it there because it still weighs the same as it did when you saw it as a table—besides which you'd better look damn quick because matter explodes at infinite density. I'd call that phenomenal.

If I tell a physicist that I have 20/20 vision and he says to me, great, that's wonderful, 20/20 lets you see point something percent of the total electromagnetic spectrum now bombarding this room, that makes my 20/20 seem like a paltry effort at apprehending reality.

Can you see, the same guy asks me, the X rays, cosmic rays, gamma rays, microwaves, radio and television broadcasts that are dancing all about us? No—but if you'll let me switch on the television, maybe I can. . . . Not good enough, he says; that is still just a fraction of the total spectrum. It's all here, right now, passing over, under, around, and even right through us—can't you see it? Well, no, not really but . . . There!—did you see that free electron that was just knocked out of its orbit around a helium nucleus by that neutrino from Upsa Vagabondi (umpty-million light-years away)—and did you see the helium atom then decay into hydrogen?

Of course not. I see the wall, the table, your face— that's 20/20 to me and to all of us who share this particular parcel of reality. The point is, there is always much more there than most of us ordinarily perceive. So don't get bent out of shape with me when I say to you that I saw something that appears to exist in a different parcel. My physicist sees that sort of thing all the time—using, of course, special tools that enable him to get a better glimpse of total reality than you and I.

Okay. Apparently I, too, have some sort of special tool buried somewhere in my skull. I do not know how it got there and I really do not know how to operate the darned thing. It comes on all by itself, gives me a glimpse that I could not get otherwise, then shuts down. I have nothing to do with it, no control whatever, and I have not the faintest idea what it is, how it works, or why it works. I have spent the better part of life wondering about it and . . .

But enough of that for now. I am just trying to give you an understanding of what *phenomenon* means to me, personally. It means, simply, anything not ordinarily perceived via the human sensory apparatus.

I saw an apparition, an "appearance," some energy form that did not have atomic structures packed into it as densely as mine are packed into me. If you prefer to call it a ghost, go ahead. For myself, I am much more comfortable trying to relate that particular type of phenomenon to some sort of psychic energy. That keeps my feet planted on solid(!) earth while I try to understand what is happening in my little parcel of reality.

At the moment in question I had enough solid-earth problems on hand without looking for more in rarer atmospheres. Karen Highland absolutely fell apart when Bruno died. She apparently had no family, no close friends, absolutely no one to turn to—and the same for Bruno. I could not just send the lady toddling along Pacific Coast Highway, all starey-eyed and terrified and totally alone in the world. She seemed convinced that "something evil" had done in Bruno and I had the impression that she was a bit worried for herself too.

I gave her a sedative and put her to bed at my place. Then I went looking for Bruno.

I found him in a refrigerated room at County. I did not even know the guy's family name, but they had all that from personal papers found in his wallet. The name, by the way, was Valensa. The "person to notify in case of an emergency" was Karen Highland, ditto for "name of employer." The home address and telephone number were the same as I had in my book for Karen.

Well, she had said that Bruno was "like an uncle."

The tag on the remains simply read "DOA"—without further comment.

I called an acquaintance at the coroner's office and told her what little I knew about Bruno Valensa and the circumstances of his death. I also said that I was acting on behalf of Karen Highland and requesting an autopsy at the earliest possible time. The coroner's assistant promised to pierce the bureaucratic veil and get something happening immediately; I, in turn, promised to call her soon for dinner.

She also suggested that I touch base with the cops. I did not feel like doing that at the moment. I had already been away for a couple of hours, and I was a bit uneasy about my new housemate. It was now about five o'clock and the traffic situation was frantic. I stopped at a little market for a few groceries, got home about six.

Uneasy, yeah, with good reason. Her car was still there. The clothing she had worn was there, folded neatly at the foot of the bed. Water was running in the shower, but the bathroom door stood wide open and no one was there—damp spot on the carpet—one large bath towel missing.

My place is not that large; took me all of thirty seconds to shake it down and to realize that I was the only one at home. I found her about a mile down the beach, wrapped in the towel, sarong fashion, walking aimlessly through ankle-deep surf. Her eyes were sort of blank. I was not positive that she knew where she was or that she even recognized me. But she took my hand like a trusting child and allowed me to lead her back to my place. We had no conversation. I put her to bed again and called my doctor. We are drinking buddies. He came out, took her temperature, and did the vital signs bit, asked her a few routine questions to which she responded in a monotone—name, rank, serial number, that sort of stuff.

Outside, he told me that she seemed healthy and rather archly inquired if we'd been "doing any stuff." He meant drugs, and he knew better. I told him about the sedative. Said I should just keep an eye on her, let her sleep it off.

By now it is nine o'clock or so. I go back inside to check her out, hoping she's asleep. She is not. She has the bedcovers kicked back and she is naked. I stand in the doorway and the dialogue is at that distance. She speaks first.

"Are you going to do it?"

"Am I going to do what, Karen?"

"You know. Give me an orgasm."

"If I could, sure. I'd do that. But that is not something someone else can give you, babe. You have to go get it for yourself. Maybe I could help you with that. Let's talk about it tomorrow."

Which shows you what a nice guy I really am. I was looking at heaven. But the moment was all wrong, the rationale was wrong—and I was not all that sure that it was the real Karen Highland in my bed. The eyes were still sort of blank, as though no one was home there.

"Tomorrow? Promise?"

"Promise, yeah, we'll talk about it."

"Is Bruno really dead?"

"Yes."

"What can I do?"

"About Bruno? Not a thing, kid. Unless there's someone I should notify."

"No. Bruno is the last—there's no one. He had a brother. Like him."

"Like him?"

"You know. Mute. He died too. Year ago, 'bout. Same way."

"Same way?"

"Yes. Here one moment, gone the next."

"We'll talk about that tomorrow."

"Kiss me good night?"

"God, no."

Something moved within those blank eyes and she giggled. "See you tomorrow, then."

I was closing the door when she very sleepily informed me, "She came for him too."

"What?"

"Tony, Bruno's brother. She came for him last year."

I went straight to the bar and made a drink, took it outside to watch a great orange moon rise into the sky—seeking, I guess, confirmation of an ordered reality.

So there I stood, whiskey and soda in hand, feet planted trustingly upon a whirling cinder that moved in endless circles around a nuclear fire in the sky, watching another cinder or ash or whatever whirling around my cinder, seeking reason and logic in an incomprehensible universe.

What fools we mortals be.

CHAPTER THREE
Falling, Falling

I spent the larger part of that night tiptoeing about in repeated checks on my guest while also playing code games with my personal computer.

Even with the strong sedative, her sleep was restless and punctuated with muffled little outcries, but I elected to let her sleep it out without interference from me; sometimes that is best.

Besides which, I was having a devil of a time with my computer linkage to the world brain. Amazing what you can do with these little gadgets—the so-called "personal computer"—if you know the tricks—and, of course, I had learned most of those under navy tutelage. It's a modest investment in "linkage." Smart shopping can set you up proudly for just a few thousand dollars, allowing you to tap in to the monster system costing millions.

A word or two is needed here about "monster systems," in case you have not noticed any. Modern human society is highly complex, much more so than one would imagine from casual observations of the common, workaday world; so complex, in fact, that it is only marginally manageable and—from an inside view—appears to be in daily danger of total collapse.

The whole thing is held together by a tenuous network of "management systems" and "data parameters" that embrace the full spectrum of government and private sector interests, most of which operate at cross-purposes and with a notable lack of cooperative effort. That the thing works at all is a testament not to the ingenuity of man but to the stubbornness of some impelling force of evolution that somehow keeps things stumbling along despite all efforts to frustrate it.

If that sounds cynical, then call me a cynic, but I am not really cynical about mankind per se, only about the mechanisms that are trying to stick us all together in manageable clumps. The mechanism has to be there, mind you, else all is chaos—witness modern Lebanon as an example of what happens when the machine collapses—but chaos is an inherent and basic constituent of every management system ever devised, more and more so as complexities increase.

I include any and every form of political government in the definition of "management systems." Include also, if you will, every religious and educational and commercial endeavor of mankind. Keep that in mind, please, then consider that the computer age has ushered in the most beautifully complex mechanisms yet conceived by an exploding race consciousness—while concomitantly producing the most menacing potential for utter chaos.

Artificial intelligence.

Sound like something from a science fiction movie? Sure, but it is also military-industrial jargon that you might encounter any Sunday in the L.A. *Times* classifieds under "Scientific Help Wanted." Artificial intelligence is the newest of the growth and glamour technological pursuits of our space-age society—mostly in military applications at the present state of development, but it has already crept into various private enterprises. The very term implies that more is under contemplation than mere data-mashing, which is mainly what a computer does; it suggests some sort of silicone brain that can reason both deductively and inductively, make decisions and execute them—the real-life equivalent of the old (ten years ago, I guess, is old by present standards) science fiction themes concerning the domination of mankind by monster computers.

But I digress. I was trying to make the point that our highly complex society of today is being managed, in most parts that really count, by computer technology and "artificial intelligence." A lot of the chaos that erupts in our personal lives, and in our personal interactions with a computer-managed society, is caused when an individual or an action does not match some mathematical model that is attempting to orchestrate the social conventions in a given sphere of activity.

I am trying not to sound professorial, but I think round so I guess I have to talk that way. Really what I am trying to suggest is that the monster computer is already among us, governing us to a large extent that we are being governed, controlling us to a large extent that we are being controlled.

I tend to resent that.

All of which, above, is a roundabout way of saying that I feel no pangs of conscience in using that same mechanism as a service to help me hold chaos at bay while I attempt some useful task.

So, yeah, I play the code games. Not in a frivolous sense, and I do have a rather stern ethic that keeps me from mucking around where I have no business. Most of the data pools that I have accessed from my little TRS-80 contain public records, anyway. Only occasionally have I invaded confidential files, and then only when the need seemed to justify the trespass.

The lady had come to me for help. If I am a physician and you come to me complaining of a bellyache and I suspect that your appendix is trying to explode, am I ethically justified in giving you a Rolaids and sending you on your way simply because you will not acknowledge the appendicitis? No—I cannot work that way.

Karen Highland had a problem that was much more ominous than the complaint that brought her to me. I did not exactly know the parameters of that problem, but I felt that I owed it to her as well as to myself to find out all I could about her.

I hit every major data bank in the state in that pursuit.

Know what? I found nothing. Nothing.

The mechanism that sticks together the people of California had no knowledge of the lady; she did not exist in that system. No driver's license, no work record, not even a record of birth, no medical records, no police records. Apparently she had never been insured, had never gone to school, never married or divorced, never applied for credit, never bought real estate, never paid taxes.

Along about three A.M., I began to get the feeling that I was falling toward chaos.

I have a distinct distaste for chaos. So I shut down the computer, took off my shoes, and stretched out on the couch to give my right brain a shot at the logic.

Instead, I guess I fell asleep because the next thing I knew, sunlight was streaming through the windows and my home had been invaded by a number of energetic men with nasty faces, two of whom were peering down at me over gun snouts.

I moved eyes and mouth only in a cautious query as to the nature of their business there.

One snapped, "Shut up."

Another, outside my area of vision, announced, "She's in here!"—and I was aware of energetic movements in the general direction of my bedroom.

It happened faster than I can describe the action. One moment they were there, the next they were gone—and Karen Highland too. I heard several vehicles pull away before I ventured to my feet. It could have been a dream for all the evidence left behind.

Even Karen could have been a dream.

But I knew that she was not.

For some strange reason, maybe only to validate the reality, the first thing I did was to call my friend at the coroner's office. It was a Saturday, but I knew that she normally worked the weekends. But she was not there, would not be there at all today, something about a family emergency out of town somewhere, no idea when she would be returning to duty.

The people at the county hospital kept me on hold for upwards of ten minutes before firmly assuring me that there was "no record" of my DOA.

Falling, yeah. Chaos loomed.

The 911 supervisor could find no record of a dispatch to my address on the previous day, and a telephone canvass of ambulance companies serving the area produced a solid ditto.

Then and only then I tried the telephone number that Karen Highland had given me just three days earlier. What I reached was a telephone company recording advising me that the number was no longer in service.

How I hate chaos.

So I called my drinking buddy, the doctor who had come over to check out Karen the evening before.

I bullied my way through two "services" to finally acquire a female voice that sorrowfully informed me that my friend, the doctor, had died of an apparent heart attack "late last night."

Someone or something was manipulating my little corner of reality, I was sure of that.

Or else the system, the social mechanism, had reached the edge of chaos and was about to engulf me in its collapse.

I could not buy that.

So I did something that could get me a few years in Leavenworth. I went back to my TRS-80 and accessed a government mainframe in Washington to invade confidential files in search of a "Highland" with a promising profile.

It took me up past the noon hour, and I was glad it was a weekend, with most of Washington away from the office, to afford me that kind of time on the access.

But, yeah, I found the "right" Highland.

And a hell of a lot more.

I found my validation. And a new respect for the mechanism.

CHAPTER FOUR
Kingdom Come

You hear a lot about Bel Air, but few people ever actually see the place. It is perhaps the most exclusive residential neighborhood in greater Los Angeles, occupies a walled area directly across Sunset from UCLA, home to the very rich. Not that every home in there is an out-and-out mansion, but even the most modest would be valued into seven figures.

The particular estate I was contemplating that Saturday afternoon more likely ran into eight figures. The confines of this minikingdom were set off behind a high stone wall. The palace, itself, appeared to consist of two stories of stone and ivy with stately rooflines, occupying probably an acre of its own. I could spot the roofs of several smaller structures buried in the trees and I could imagine the rest: luxury pool, maybe a tennis court or two, several acres of lawn and flowers, lots of exotic shrubbery.

In a neighborhood of the very rich, the Highland estate quietly proclaimed its status among the superrich.

I was impressed.

But I would have been surprised to find less after my morning foray into confidential government files.

Joseph Highland, at his death, had been one of the richest men in the world. The full extent of his personal fortune could only be estimated, even by his own accountants. The estate had been in probate for more than ten years and still all the numbers were not in.

The founder of this kingdom seemed to have had fingers into just about every big pie in the world, and a fist or two into some of the hottest ones—transportation, motion pictures, petroleum, commodities of every sort, electronics, aviation, international banking on a grand scale, stocks and bonds to dazzle the mind, insurance, on and on; the list seemed endless.

Apparently he had been a very private man, almost secretive, running his worldwide business empire from behind those very walls, seldom venturing physically into the world beyond—a shadowy figure who never publicly attached his name to his holdings—that name actually concealed at great lengths beneath layer upon layer of corporate identities, never appearing on social registers or listed in connection with the various philanthropic foundations in which he was heavily involved.

Heavily, yeah—old Joe Highland had given away more than a billion bucks just during the final ten years of his life. That much, at least, was documented.

The official record—what I could find of it—revealed but one marriage and one child, a son—

Thomas James Highland—who seemed to have been as reclusive as his father and who had, himself, expired within a year of the death of the father.

Karen, it seemed, was Thomas's only child, Joseph's granddaughter and sole heir to all that mentioned above.

That understanding had jarred me, bringing forth a dozen or more fanciful scenarios to explain the unsettling events of the previous twenty-four hours. And I was glad that I had not overreacted to that latest event starring Karen Highland, heiress to an international financial empire. I would have had a sweet time trying to establish a "kidnapping" from my beach cottage of a lady who apparently did not exist in the official system, and an even sweeter time after a supposed police trail led to this palace in Bel Air.

That kind of money also spells power of a very special kind—a power that ordinary citizens seldom get a sniff of—the kind of which you and I, pal, do not wish to run afoul.

Not that I was running scared. It just seemed logical, to me, that a Karen Highland—any Karen Highland, by any other name—would enjoy (or suffer) a rather elaborate security system that could not tolerate aimless wanderings about the countryside and/or casual overnight flops here and there.

It seemed obvious to me, in that hindsight, that Bruno Valensa had been Karen's personal bodyguard, that he'd probably accompanied her everywhere outside the palace—and I could picture the consternation at home when the princess failed to arrive at a reasonable time and the bodyguard turned up dead at the county morgue.

I was considering myself fortunate that those guys had not marched me into the surf and ordered me to swim to Catalina with my hands bound behind me.

But there are scenarios and scenarios.

I had to at least see the lady in her natural habitat and satisfy myself that she was in good hands. Then I would run, not walk, to the nearest exit and leave the entire experience happily behind me.

Didn't work out that way.

The guy at the gatehouse gave me no trouble whatever. I identified myself, told him I was calling on Miss Highland. He relayed my name by intercom to the house or somewhere and I was passed right on through with maybe a ten-second delay, all told.

Which gave me a funny feeling. Had I been expected to show up here? Who was behind the cadre of bodyguards or whatever that had invaded my home that morning with such damned arrogance—waving guns, yet—and what the hell was I walking into here.

Hey—I've seen the same movies you've seen about the poor dear heiress dominated and manipulated by greedy scoundrels trying to do her out of her megabucks. Stuff like that, fiction or not, sticks in the mind—maybe because we all at least subconsciously recognize the fact that art imitates life, that there is some basis in reality for fictional drama.

So I was a bit uneasy, sure, I don't mind saying so, but that feeling was very quickly overpowered by another. My initial, outside impression of that palace could not match the inside reality. My Maserati felt right at home amid all that splendor as it tooled along the wide, curving drive toward the house, past seas of flowers and immaculate flagstone pathways, over tumbling brooks with waterfalls and living swans, exotic flowering trees dotting acres of rolling lawn—but that Maserati had always seemed smugly superior to me, as though she knew I really could not afford her, and frankly I felt a bit out of place, definitely uncomfortable, perhaps smarting just a bit from the memory of my protective instincts toward the mistress of such a joint. In short, the reality of Highlandville put me in my place, reminding me that, after all, a movie is just a movie, but life is a bowl of cherries.

I almost turned around and went right back out, but I resisted the impulse, set my jaw, and sallied on.

Glad I did.

Something was going on there. Twenty or so cars were parked beyond the portico and a uniformed attendant was standing ready to receive mine. I told the guy, no, thanks, nobody drives the Maserati but me, and I took her on through and placed her carefully beside a Rolls.

A guy in a waiter's uniform looked me over as I quit the Maserati, apparently deciding that my tennis shorts and polo shirt qualified me as a guest, in contrast to a service person, because he gave me a friendly smile as I approached and directed me toward an area behind the house.

A party was in progress back there—several couples of the beautiful set lounging beside the pool in skimpy swimwear and chatting amiably, several others hoisting drinks at an island bar, two couples playing cards at a poolside table—all in swimsuits or otherwise scantily clad. The only guy there wearing long pants and shoes was bare from the waist up; this one saw me coming and trotted over to intercept me at the edge of the lawn.

"You're Ford?" he asked casually, with a smile. Before I could confirm that, he went on to say, "Toby told me he was sending you on up. Glad you could make it. We all want to thank you for taking such good care of Karen last night. Kid had us worried to death."

He stuck out a hand and I shook it courteously as he kept right on talking without a pause, but I would have liked to tell him that the guys with the guns had already conveyed the gratitude of the kingdom. This guy looked about forty-five or maybe a young fifty, it would be hard to say, very smooth veneer covering a tough-as-nails personality, kind of guy you'd expect to see at the head of the table at a board meeting of some megabuck corporation—all self-assured, a touch superior and more than a touch condescending behind that facade of chatty amiability.

"I'm Terry Kalinsky," as though I should immediately know what that meant. "That's my wife, Marcia—" He was indicating a tall, blond woman of roughly his own age, still very pretty and sexy in a one-half-ounce bikini, seated on the diving board with a cocktail. "—and I'll let you make your own introductions to the others, we don't stand on formalities here. Karen should be along in a few minutes, I sent word that you were here, meanwhile why don't you try the bar and just sort of mellow in. Uh, you want to try the tennis court later—" He was noticing my shorts. "—I'm sure you could scare up a partner, maybe even some mixed doubles. I'd go for that, keep me in mind."

Kalinsky walked away and left me standing there with my mouth poised for speech and nary a word uttered. He'd not even heard the sound of my voice, and the impression was clear that he felt no loss from that.

I wandered to the bar and was trying to massage the guy through my mind with a whiskey and soda, also trying to get the drift of what the hell was going on here in the very shadow of the recent intrigue.

The "kid" may have had them "worried to death" last night, but the recovery from that seemed complete—so on with the games, eh?

Or, I thought, maybe I was overplaying the thing in my own mind. But then there was Bruno and his missing corpse, the flying squad at my house, all that damned ruckus—for what?

And who the hell was Kalinsky?

Maybe I was about to find out. His wife was approaching, eyes fixed on me in an openly curious stare, swaying along in the exaggerated movements of a cultured woman who has been taught to walk properly, even barefoot in a bikini, but with the motor nerves influenced by too many pulls at the cocktail shaker.

I smiled and made room for her at the bar, but she kept on moving, until one bare hip was nestled against mine. The voice was quietly pleasant, well modulated despite the same type of motor-nerve interference, just a touch of humor or maybe tease. "So. And just who are you, my lovely?"

I did not take it badly. Some people just come on that way—some people like these, especially. I'd traveled these crowds before. Not quite this rare, but close enough that I was not intimidated by Marcia Kalinsky.

I gave her my name and nothing else, figuring that should suffice since they-all had been so wanting to thank me for taking care of the kid last night.

But apparently the name meant nothing whatever to this one, right away placing her outside the circle of "we all."

"I'm Ashton Ford, Mrs. Kalinsky."

"What is an Ashton Ford—something like a Model-T?"

I laughed politely. What the hell—why not? "Not exactly. Nice party." That gave me an excuse to break the stare-down and glance about at the others.

"It's a rotten party. Same bunch every Saturday. I'm sick of them." That bare hip was pressing closer in a reminder that it was there. "I'm ready for a real party, skinny-dipping in the pool, all that good stuff—you know?"

I knew. And I had to get away from that inviting hip. Besides which, it appeared that an ample bosom was in imminent danger of defeating the few threads restraining it, and I have never really learned to act cool in such an emergency.

But there was a diversion, of sorts, at the edge of

things; another group of guests was arriving, moving noisily in from the parking area.

Also, and at the same moment, the princess herself—Karen Highland—presented herself at poolside.

She was stark, staring naked and walking directly toward me.

About halfway there, she lofted ahead a greeting in clear, sweet tones. "Ashton! How wonderful!"

By this time she is at my side, the other side opposite bare hip, clasping my hand warmly and raising it overhead in some sort of triumphant gesture.

"Look, everyone! This is Ashton! My sex surrogate! He has kindly consented to give me an orgasm!"

Everyone, it seemed, was just staring at us rather stupidly. The silence, for a moment there, was thunderous.

Then Marcia Kalinsky blurted, "God's sake, Karen! You've lost your suit!"

Whereupon "the kid" seemed to rouse from some weird form of waking trance, looked down at her naked self in absolute horror, dropped my hand as though it were a firebrand, and bolted back into the sanctuary of her palace.

It was at about that moment, I believe, that I began thinking about Karen Highland in terms of double habitation.

CHAPTER FIVE
Body and Soul

If you have never heard the term "double habitation," and I would suppose that many well-informed people have not, it refers to a peculiar and really quite rare human situation in which a single body seems to be host to two separate personalities. There are cases recorded involving multiple habitation. The shrinks talk about it in terms of a schizophrenic manifestation—split-personality, dissociation, etc.— but other learned people with equally valid credentials prefer to see it as something else.

The opposing poles of thought are best exemplified in the public mind by a couple of motion picture dramas—with the psychiatric view presented in *The Three Faces of Eve,* the story of a woman whose personality was split into three distinct and disparate identities; the other view given the widest public exposure by *The Exorcist,* the supernatural story of a young girl possessed by a demonic spirit.

Not being credentialed either way, I had always felt free to make my own conclusions, though I had never done so because I had never really been faced with the need to do so.

I did have the opportunity a couple of years ago to study some video footage of a young man in the San Francisco area who appeared to exhibit five different personalities, only two of which were male—and I ran into a guy at Big Sur last year who slipped over into an identity as Alexander the Great when faced with a difficult problem beyond his immediate abilities. This guy, when in one of these "spells," held one-sided conversations with none other than Aristotle, in a strange tongue that I am told is Classical Greek.

I did not have any clear idea as to what any of this might have to do with Karen Highland or her strange behavior, but I was rather impressed by the way Kalinsky reacted to that stunning stunt. His wife had run on behind Karen and followed her inside the house, pausing at the doorway to snatch up a terry cloth robe that apparently had been abandoned there.

Some of the ladies present were shooting me guardedly measuring looks. Mainly, though, everyone was just standing about in giggly-embarrassed clusters, wondering maybe if this meant that the party was over.

Enter Kalinsky, then, moving casually from group to group, grinning and talking a mile a minute, putting the guests at ease. By the time he got to me, everything seemed just about back to where it had been before.

He strolled past me with the same grin he'd worn

for the others, but the vocal tone was tailored just for me as he delivered his orders without breaking stride: "We need to talk."

I left my unfinished drink at the bar and gladly followed his unhurried tracks across the patio and into the house. Entry there was via a large lounge area—for want of a better name; I'd almost call it a nightclub. A full bar that would be the envy of many commercial clubs occupied an entire wall. A dozen or so heavy leather couches arranged with marble tables and computer games still left plenty of room for a decent dance floor and a small, raised stage outfitted with grand piano, drums, amplifiers, and whatnot. Two guys who looked the bartender role were working stock behind the bar and apparently getting set up for a long evening. Otherwise, the lounge was deserted.

We went on through there and along a bright hallway past another room, which could have lobbied for a small resort hotel, before Kalinsky spoke to me again.

This time it was over the shoulder as he veered left into another, broader hallway with doors spaced along either side. "Executive wing," he told me, with the air of a bored tour guide.

"Naturally," I replied, but under my breath.

We were, it seems, at the seat of government. One of the rooms we passed—actually a broader hall teed off behind an archway and sealed in glass—had OPERATIONS CENTER engraved in gold on the double glass doors. In smaller letters below: Authorized Personnel Only.

I marked that one in the mind but had only a quick study as we walked past: no windows, big mainframe computer at the back wall, several small desks with terminals, half a dozen or so Teletypes and several stockmarket tickers, God knows what else. This was Saturday afternoon, remember, but two of the Teletypes were spitting copy and a guy in knee shorts and bright Hawaiian shirt was wrestling a stack of computer printouts.

The throne room was at the very end, beyond another ten or twelve closed-door offices, with its own waiting room with two secretarial desks and a telephone switchboard—the old PBX type.

Kalinsky trailed a finger along the top of the switchboard as we walked through—said, almost lovingly, "Don't use this anymore, of course, but it was JQ's pride so we keep it around for old time's sake."

I learned later that everyone at the palace referred to the dead king by his initials (middle name was Quincy). The also-dead son was called TJ, when at all.

Seemed to be the style here to abbreviate names. Kalinsky murmured, "In here, Ash," as he showed me into the Executive Office.

I don't know exactly what I'd been expecting to find in there, but it must have been less than the reality because I was a bit surprised by the layout. The polished mahogany desk (Philippine mahogany, no doubt) would hold a king-size mattress, even between the swirls for the visitors' chairs, which were pedestal-mounted on swivel bases and richly upholstered in some fine leather. The executive chair, rail-mounted at the rear, was contour-molded and heavily padded with a backrest about four feet high. Had a control console built into the right armrest—I didn't know, maybe they launched missiles from Vandenberg here—and there was another gizmo built into the desk that obviously was light-years ahead of the old PBX in the outer office, some jazzy telephone setup with video monitors and taping facilities.

Kalinsky motioned me toward one of the three scoop-outs up front. Pretty nice working environment, I had to admit as I eased myself into the imbedded chair—imbedded in the desk, that is, at just the proper height to rest both arms on the shiny surface at either side, plenty of work space directly ahead, each chair angled into the massive structure in such a way that four people could be seated there and working comfortably while almost head to head.

I took the opportunity to orient myself as Kalinsky went around and clambered into the Command Pilot's seat. Nice, yeah, very impressive. About forty feet square, interior walls displaying heavy books from floor to ceiling, French windows opening onto a private flower garden and outside lounge, luxurious carpeting, evidence of a tiled bath off behind the desk—probably very elaborate—all the usual tycoon comforts and then some.

"I'd offer you a drink, but JQ was death on mixing booze with business—so, no drinking in the executive wing—I'm sure you understand—we still honor JQ here."

I said, "Sure. Not that much for booze, myself."

"Good. Nothing against a social drink, mind you."

"'Course not," I agreed.

All that dispensed, my host was now obviously ready to get to that talk we both needed.

"We know exactly who you are, of course."

That was nice. I was not sure, myself, exactly who I was. But I knew, now, approximately who Kalinsky was. There was no doubt in my mind that he was the "we" who was now running this empire.

"We got your pedigree. Shortly after you got Bruno."

"Poor guy," I said quietly.

"Yeah. You shouldn't have copped the poor guy in the balls, you know."

"He didn't die of that," I observed.

"How do you know that? Delayed reaction, maybe."

"Are you suggesting that's where his heart was?"

The guy chuckled. It was not a bad sound. But we were, after all, discussing a recently dead employee and organizational "uncle."

"Sometimes I wondered," Kalinsky said, still grinning. The smile faded as he veered back into our talk. "I was not referring to his unfortunate death. But that was a shock, a real shock, too young for that. I meant after he came home with bruised balls. I gave him hell, too, for putting himself in that position. And for putting Karen in that position."

"Not the name of the game," I agreed.

"Absolutely not. That girl is—well . . . you know. We all are trying to help her through this."

I said, "Naturally."

"Sure. Could be very damaging, very . . . scandalous, degrading. I mean to the family name as well as to herself, and we all are . . ."

". . . trying to help her through this," I helped.

"Naturally," he replied, turning it back to me.

I was beginning to like the guy, though with strong reservations. Or maybe *respect* is a better tag for what I was feeling at that moment.

I said, "Let's get back to Bruno. Where's the body?"

"In a funeral chapel, where it belongs."

I said, "But, naturally, to help him get through that . . ."

Kalinsky chuckled again. I believe he was starting to like me too. "Pretty sharp, aren't you? Look, Ash, this family does not need notoriety."

This "family," I was thinking as he continued talking, now consisted of a single person: Karen.

"JQ would have done it this way. I was a punk kid fresh out of Harvard Business School when he took me under his wing, wet as hell behind the ears and not a dime to call my own. He gave me the responsibility for Karen, and by God I mean to exercise it the same way he would. So don't miscalculate my feelings in all this. She is my granddaughter, dammit, the same as if . . ."

"Grandfather surrogate," I mused. "But you're far too young."

A slow smile began at his eyes and spread warmly toward his mouth as he pushed that one around. "Better than—I thought I'd die. But it was funny, wasn't it? I mean—serious, sure, serious and embarrassing as hell, but still funny. Wonder whatever possessed her to pull something like that."

"Exactly," I said.

"Exactly, to what?"

"Whatever possessed her."

"Don't get you."

"It wasn't Karen."

"What do you mean, it wasn't Karen?"

"Not herself."

"Oh. Sure. 'Course not. That's what made it so damned funny. But she's been doing a lot of strange stuff lately, and . . ."

"Ever see her like that before?"

"Like what?"

"Naked."

"Oh. Well . . ."

"Grandfatherly fashion, of course."

I got a flash from the eyes as he responded to that one. "I was thinking of when she was a little girl—but, no, nothing like that since—hold it, there, Ash—why do I feel that you've taken charge of this conversation?"

I showed him a flash of my own as I replied, "You said 'Have a talk.' Talk flows both ways, doesn't it?"

The lord of the manor produced a single cigarette and lit it without offering me one. I took the opportunity to study him closely while he did so, then I lit one of my own.

He was less relaxed than when we came in there, shoulders a bit tight and tilted forward—aggression—chin out and reaching toward the flame as he lit up—belligerence—fingers clenched tightly onto the cigarette—fear of losing—hard, sharp pulls as he sucked up the smoke—anxious—settling back in his chair to fix me with a stern gaze—reasserting control.

"Didn't like the navy life, eh?"

I blew smoke back across the desk to mingle with his and replied, "Too confining. Great institution, though, if you like institutions."

"But you don't."

"Not usually."

"Maverick. Love your independence. Like to run your own show. Can't really knuckle under to organizational structures."

I showed him a very small smile and replied, "Bingo."

"IQ of one-ninety. That's genius level."

I waved it aside. "Genius is as genius does, or however that goes. I never put much stock in intelligence tests."

"Trust fund from your mother's family really doesn't set you up the way you'd like to be, though. You can't afford that Maserati, Ash."

Bingo, again, but I would not give him the satisfaction. "I do okay. Lots of sun, plenty of fresh air, come and go as I please. Why are you hiding Bruno's body?"

He did not miss a beat. "Who says we're hiding it and why should we? Fella has a right to a decent laying-out. Simply had him removed to a decent place."

"You removed also every official trace of the event."

"The vulgar press loves this kind of shit. We just do what has to be done to avoid notoriety."

"JQ would have done it that way."

"Bet your ass. And, speaking of your ass, my friend, you really had no right to push the coroner that way, desecrate the body, all that shit. Man died a natural death. Leave him alone in peace. Why don't you become a tennis pro?"

He was showing me that he could turn it quickly too. I was really beginning to enjoy this. "Think I'm good enough?"

"Beat the shit out of Centrales at Carmel. Yeah, I'd call that good enough."

The guy really had my number. And I could tell that he was enjoying calling it too.

I wagged the cigarette at him, then snuffed it out as I told him, "This is one reason why not. You're right. I like my independence, even to the point of choosing my own poisons. Professional athletics are too rigorous."

"You don't like rigor."

"We already covered that. I do not like rigor. And that, I suppose, is why I should be leaving you right about now." But I made no move to go.

He said, "You're a good team player, though. Navy thought so. Bet they cried when you left them."

I said, "Karen is in severe difficulty."

He said, "I know that. What the hell do you think we're talking about?"

I saw his hand move on the armrest, a finger poising over the buttons of the console, then selecting one by feel.

I thought, oh shit, it's a James Bond movie and now I am about to plunge through this floor into a pit of hungry crocodiles.

But nothing like that happened. And Kalinsky went right on talking. "This really isn't my style, but I have to tell you that I like you, Ash. I guess I really expected it to go this way. I mean, I figured we'd get along fine even before I finished reading your file. This little talk really just confirms everything I expected to find. Look, we've tried everything with this kid and now we're really beginning to feel desperate. Mind you, I don't usually show my hand this way, but I guess you know already the trouble we've got. So even if you weren't worth a shit I'd rather have you on the inside than outside somewhere raising a lot of notoriety."

The guy seemed really hung up on "notoriety"—a holdover, I presumed, from the JQ brand of public relations.

Knuckles rapped lightly on the paneled door behind me and a guy glided silently in, placed a manila file folder in Kalinsky's right hand, then glided back out without a glance at me.

"Something here I want you to look over. Study it carefully and make sure you understand the full ramifications before deciding either way." He removed an officious-looking document on legal-size paper and slid it across the polished surface of the desk.

It was an employment contract, several pages of it, with maybe five lines relating what I would get and the rest laboriously detailing what they would get.

Right up front, for me, was two grand a day plus full living and business expenses with a thirty-day minimum, payable in advance, renewable in thirty-day chunks at the pleasure of the employer. A check for the first sixty thousand was attached, made out to me, awaiting only a signature to make it operative.

One little scrawl on a piece of paper and I would be, right up front, worth almost as much as my Maserati.

I guess my eyes reacted a bit at that figure because Kalinsky chuckled quietly and threw in a clincher.

"Of course you will be immediately issued all the most powerful plastic to cover outside expenses, all billed directly to the corporation. You'll never even have to know how much you're taking us for, so the salary is free and clear."

The salary, yeah, but how free and clear would I be with someone buying me in thirty-day chunks in advance?

I read on.

It was a body-and-soul contract. They would own me, twenty-four hours a day and by the month. I would sleep at their pleasure, eat and drink and make merry at their pleasure—and, I presumed, kill and maim and screw at their pleasure.

Two basically operative phrases recurred over and over: " . . . at the pleasure of the employer . . . " and " . . . without regard to employee's personal conscience."

There was a covenant on loyalty, one on secrecy, several more to cover any paranoid threat to " . . . the public image, safety, and general well being of the employer."

They even got my body if I died on duty—and I right away transposed that into the situation with Bruno.

At the bottom appeared what is sometimes referred to as a closed-loop option; they had a binder on my life, forever, renewable at their pleasure every thirty days but never at mine.

I glanced at Kalinsky and said, "The way JQ did it, eh?"

He said, "Always. You want to argue with the success of it?"

I replied, "Depends on the point of view. Success for whom?"

"It's a standard contract. We all work under the same requirements, all of us here. The only difference is the salary. And that is never negotiable. You take the whole deal or none of it."

"You can't really hold people to this option. Not in this country. If a guy wants to leave . . ."

"The hell we can't. We can't physically restrain him, no—can't make him stay if he's dead set on leaving. Can sure as hell make him wish he had, though. He'll never work anywhere else, for anybody, at any price, not even for himself. So think about it before you sign. Think about this, too, though. We already consider you under our influence. Can't let you walk away from it now. So, whether you sign or not, we consider that we nevertheless own a moral option, and we will enforce it."

I carefully lay the thing on the desk while quietly

musing, "Some American Indian tribe had this peculiar custom . . . you save a guy's life . . . then he owns you forever."

Kalinsky grinned amiably. "Exactly."

I said, "Bullshit."

"Better think about it."

"How long?"

"Midnight."

"Tonight," I presumed.

He was still grinning, enjoying it. "Midnight tonight. I guess your only decision, Ash, is are we friends or enemies. As friends, we can be very nice. As enemies . . ."

"Another story comes to mind," I said quietly. "One about this guy who sells his soul to the devil."

"Devil has all the options, Ash. I'm surprised you didn't know that. It's written in original sin."

"JQ say that?"

"He did."

I said, and meant it, "Bullshit."

CHAPTER SIX

Conjunction

I do not mind saying that I was more than a little disturbed by Kalinsky's attitude toward my life and liberty. The guy sat there with a grin on his face and as much as told me that he was taking me over, like it or not—as though I were an open-stock corporation and he was buying up all the shares.

The money was great, sure, but only a pervert lives for money alone.

I would sell the Maserati before I would sign a deal like that, yet he made it quite clear that I was his, signed or not.

So I was perturbed, yes. I did not feel that he was bluffing. He meant it, every word and wink of it, and I knew that the threat was very real.

But I could see no profit in a showdown at that moment and, besides, I wanted some time with Karen before the walls came tumbling down. She was the client, Kalinsky was not, and I was not satisfied in my own mind that she was, indeed, in good hands.

So I cooled it and kept the banter going with Kalinsky until another guy came along to show me to a guest room upstairs. Seemed that a formal dinner party was brewing for the evening, some twenty to thirty additional guests, and I would be expected to "keep the kid under control" during that.

These people apparently never heard of thinking small or of finding a situation beyond their ability to manage. Believe it, a guy was waiting for me inside my room, with a mouth full of pins and a tailor's tape over the shoulder, to fit me into a tux for the occasion.

Also waiting there was an "ice-box snack," promised by Kalinsky to hold me until dinner, consisting of cold chicken, fruit, cookies, and an insulated decanter of coffee. The room boasted a fully stocked bar, complete with several different brands of imported beer and wine—had its own hi-fi, television, whirlpool bath, and outside balcony overlooking the pool. A guy could live there, sure, in total luxury, and I found myself wondering what kind of fool it took to turn down a life like this.

Maybe it would be worth the trade in personal freedom. After all, freedom to roam the wilderness all hungry and dying of thirst would not be too much of a trade for a cage with plenty of food and water. I could believe Kalinsky's assurances that my every need would be met if I would just pledge my soul to the cause. If all these people here were indeed working under "the same requirements," and I had no reason to doubt it, I had to admit that they seemed a rather contented bunch.

Of course, cows in deep pasture usually seem a rather contented bunch too; I would not trade my life for theirs.

So I ate the chicken while the tailor fussed with the fit. When he departed I headed straight for the bath, taking the coffee with me and opting for a stinging shower in preference to the lulling comfort of the whirlpool. It was past six; dinner was at eight; I wanted a moment with Karen in private before the festivities.

I tracked her down via the "Intercom Directory" and got her on the house phone. She still sounded a bit upset but in control as she invited me to her "apartment" and told me how to get there. It was on the same floor, but seemingly a half-mile distant around several bends of hallway—not too bad, except that I was wearing only a bulky shower robe (compliments of management) for the safari.

Karen was not alone. A nice-eyed man of about forty and prematurely bald, whom she introduced only as Carl, was standing in the open doorway and chatting with her when I arrived. Neither of them blinked at my get-up, maybe because the three of us were identically attired, but Karen had a bit of trouble meeting my eyes at first.

Turns out that Carl was Carl U. Powell, M.D.— house doctor and resident shrink—which explained the CUP monogrammed on the breast pocket of his robe, which in turn suggested that he was a company man "under the same requirements."

He looked me over with a not unfriendly stare,

shook my hand, and took his leave before I could really get his make and model.

Karen retreated into the depths somewhere, leaving me alone in the hallway. I went on in and closed the door, found her standing at a window in the sitting room, hands jammed tightly into the pockets of the robe, gazing fixedly onto the front lawn. It was a nice view but, again, I had the feeling that she was seeing nothing beyond her own eyeballs.

She spoke to me very quietly and without altering her position at the window. "Can you forgive me? I feel really . . . crummy."

I matched her tone and mood as I replied to that. "I suspect that you have nothing to apologize for."

She looked at me, then—just a turn of the head and a sweep with the eyes—and I could see the misery there, and I started getting mad as hell, a slow burn beginning way down low in the belly. I knew what she was feeling because I had sampled a small taste of it during the meeting with Kalinsky, a sort of formless rage lightly brushed with panic, the recognition that someone with raw power was making designs on your life-force.

I turned her about and took her in my arms, and we just stood there embracing through a long, warmly electric silence, flowing into each other, meeting somewhere in psyche and joining thoroughly in a surging transfer.

I felt her stiffen momentarily and feebly struggle against it before releasing in total surrender, mind and body, molding to me, attaching, merging. We were one body and one mind between the infinities, a

single point of reference in the space-time contin-
uum, but not moving with it, outside somewhere, out
of plane, out of body.

It shook her, shook us both, brought tears to both.

I do not know how this may sound to you—maybe
somewhat like a pride-and-passion novel, or maybe
you will just think I am kooky or melodramatic—if
you have never experienced the same thing. It was
not the first time for me, but still it was rare enough
that I found it remarkable and damned near incredi-
ble that two people—strangers, really—could spontaneously ignite into something like this, could be
transported from the workaday world into cosmic
zonk in a fingersnap.

Suddenly I knew this lady, knew all about her in
shades more intimate than anything shared by life-
long companions, knew her in her essences, her long-
ings and deepest fears and feelings, knew her in all
the sweet quiet whisperings from another star somewhere, another system, another reality.

Call it what you will; I can only report the facts.

That kind of knowing is the deepest sort of love.

And I knew, even before I pulled away and looked
into her eyes, that she knew me as I knew her,

CHAPTER SEVEN
Poor Little Rich Dreamer

We could and should have had a full-blown sexual encounter then and there, except that the circumstances of the moment were so out of kilter; Karen was in trouble, I was in trouble, maybe this entire enterprise was in trouble, and all of that was part and parcel of the understanding we'd shared out there between the infinities.

Also, the experience had been just a bit too overwhelming for her to handle all in a piece. Her knees buckled, and she would have gone down except for my support. I helped her to a couch and went for water.

She had both feet tucked under her and was dreamily contemplating an unlit cigarette when I returned. I traded her the glass for the cigarette and lit it while she sipped the water, gave her a drag, took one myself, then put it out, took a sip of water for myself.

All this time Karen was staring at me with those great, glowing eyes, raising hell with my nervous system. She had never seemed more beautiful, more appealing, more vulnerable.

I did not dare touch her. "You okay?" I inquired, trying to make it casual.

She replied with an almost imperceptible nod of the head and without detaching that gaze. "Guess so. How did you do that?"

I wished I had, and wished I knew how. I told her, "We didn't do it, it did us. Happens, sometimes, when all the ingredients are there.

"It was . . . cosmic."

I said, "Yes. I think so. The important thing is to trust it, accept it, go with it. Can you do that?"

She pondered that for a moment before replying, "I doubt that I could do otherwise. But I'm not sure I understand . . ."

I lit another cigarette, offered it to her, but she declined with a shake of the head; I said, my eyes following the spiraling trail of smoke, "You suddenly knew me. I mean, knew. Maybe as you've never, ever known another human being."

"Yes, I . . . think that's it," she said, maybe a bit confused.

"Don't let me define the experience for you."

"No, that—that's it. But more. Much more than that."

"The important thing, right now," I suggested, "is the knowing. I think maybe it is all important. You are in trouble, Karen. Maybe deep trouble. You need a friend, someone to trust. I'm asking you to give me that trust, that confidence."

She said, without a blink, "I trust you with my life, Ashton."

"It could get down to that," I muttered. "Look, you have a right to know . . . " I suddenly felt miserable, incompetent, scared. "I don't know anything about anything. All I have is feeling, belly instinct. So don't trust me with your very life, Karen. All I am asking for is your confidence that I am feeling and acting in your ultimate best interest. Please give me that and nothing more than that."

She said, very quietly, almost awed, "Okay. I understand."

I told her, "I need to know, in a word, one word, how you feel about your own life at this moment, your life situation."

"In a word," she replied, without taking time to think about it, "depressing."

"That seems very strange," I commented. "You would be the envy of almost any woman. You have youth, beauty, fabulous wealth."

"Poor little rich girl," she said grimly. "It is not what it is cracked up to be. I don't have much to relate to. I mean, with other women. With the world at large, really. This is my world, always has been. But from what I can gather, I have a terribly unnatural life-style."

"How long have you been aware of that?"

"Always, I guess," she replied quietly. "At least since I've been old enough to even know who I am. Now, sometimes, I don't even seem to know that."

"Are you frightened?"

"Do you mean right now?"

"Right now, an hour ago, yesterday, tomorrow. Are you frightened?"

"I guess I am," she replied dully.

"What frightens you?"

She seemed to be thinking about it. Quite awhile. Then: "Myself, mainly."

"Does Kalinsky frighten you?"

"Terry?" She wrinkled her nose, smiled. "His bark is worse than his bite. I think—I see him—I believe Terry is just . . . overburdened. With his own sense of responsibility, I mean. Tries too hard. Takes it all much too seriously."

"Yeah, that's how he takes it," I quietly agreed.

"I get very angry with him sometimes. He can be very stubborn and demanding. But I am not afraid of him."

"Could you fire him if you wanted to? Send him packing?"

She smiled again. "I've never really thought about it."

"Think about it now," I suggested.

"Well, he—I don't know. He's administrator of the estate. And trustee of several funds, until they come to me. I don't suppose I could change that. But . . . if you mean . . . do I have to live under the same roof with him . . . I really can't answer that."

I said, "These, uh, trust funds . . ."

"From Poppa—my grandfather. I gather that it is all very complicated—also the estate—very complicated, I mean, since my parents died very soon after Poppa. And I was a minor."

"How did your parents die?"

"A boating accident. I was fourteen."

"That's uh, tough on a kid. I'm sorry."

"I got over it," she said, almost defensively. "Never knew them all that well, anyway."

"Still . . ."

She showed me a small smile. "Well, sure, I cried for a long time. Thank God for Terry and Marcia. They were like family. I was flower girl in their wedding. So . . . well, actually, the whole staff has been like a big family. I think Poppa sort of designed it that way. I have never really felt alone in the world."

I reminded her, "You created that impression yesterday, at my place. I thought you were alone in the world, except for Bruno."

Her eyes fell. "Bruno was my good buddy," she said. "I will miss him terribly." The eyes came back up, full blaze. "I'm sorry I wasn't entirely honest with you. But after all . . . consider the circumstances."

I said, "I was not complaining, merely commenting. Sometimes, with strangers, we subconsciously reveal true feelings."

She replied, "Okay, so maybe sometimes I do really feel the role of poor little rich girl."

I asked, "Have you ever felt prisoner to all this?"

"Prisoner? I don't—no, I—my life is my own."

"Is it really?"

The eyes fell again. "I don't know," she said miserably.

I had to persist. "You've never felt mad as hell, maybe scared as hell, too, about your life situation?"

"I guess maybe I have," she admitted.

Yes, I rather guessed, too, that she had. I inquired, as casually as I could make it sound, "When do you come into the trusts?"

"On my twenty-fifth birthday," she replied, just as casually.

"And that is . . . ?"

"Next week," she said.

"Next week," I echoed, the thinking mind already occupied elsewhere. "This is Saturday, so . . . "

"One week from today. Next Saturday. Marcia has planned a huge party. I wish they'd just . . . "

"You'd rather not have a party?"

She replied, "We party every Saturday. It all seems so pointless. I'd rather spend the time meditating."

I hardly heard that. My thinking part was pounding along another trail. I asked her, "Are you frightened about next Saturday?"

"Frightened? No. Why should I be?"

"No anxiety at all?"

"No. I just don't see any point to it."

"Awhile ago, Karen, when you came downstairs, you dropped your robe at the door and walked onto the patio totally naked. Do you remember doing that?"

Her eyes clouded, dropped, inspected the hem of her robe. She said, very quietly, "Yes, of course I remember, but . . . not naked, no, I didn't think . . . "

"You believed that you were wearing something beneath the robe?"

"My bathing suit. I . . . can't explain. I thought I had put on the yellow bikini, but . . . "

"But obviously you had not."

"Obviously. It was here when I returned to the apartment, in the drawer where I usually keep it. I can't . . . "

"Do you remember the announcement you made, downstairs, when you took my hand to introduce me to your guests—do you remember what you said?"

"Yes. I remember what I said."

"Do you know why you said that?"

"Well, I—I remember—I meant—I was very happy that you had come, and . . . "

"Are you confused about this, Karen?"

"I think, yes, I am confused, I don't know why I said that. Marcia called it a Freudian slip but I—I don't think so. I mean, okay, maybe I was thinking it, but my God, I would never say something like that, not even to a best friend in confidence. No way would I slip it at the top of my voice to that crowd down there."

"What did Carl say about it?"

"No big deal, he said. Not to worry, he said. Carl is like that."

"How long has Carl been saying things like that to you?"

"He has been here about . . . five years, I guess. Yes, since shortly after my twentieth birthday. Five years."

"Isn't it a bit unusual to have a live-in doctor?"

"Is it?" She shrugged delicately. "I guess if you can afford it, why not?"

"Has there always been a doctor on staff? Or is Carl the first?"

She made a thoughtful face, said, "Poppa had one here for a while . . . I guess . . . the last year or two. He had a lot of pain, cancer. But that was the only real doctor until Carl. Several of the security men are trained as paramedics. But I don't know, does that seem unusual to you?"

I said, "A full-time doctor plus paramedics is more than many small towns have. You say Carl came just after you turned twenty?"

"About a week after my birthday, yes. I remember it because Marcia made a joke about him being a late birthday gift."

"Then he was hired primarily to doctor you?"

"Oh, I don't think so. I've never been ill."

"You said earlier that you were the Kalinsky's flower girl. When was that?"

"I must have been about five," she replied, frowning with the effort to recall. "They've been married . . . I guess close to twenty years. I believe their next anniversary is their twentieth. Unless I just dreamed the whole thing."

"What do you mean? Dreamed what whole thing?"

"About the wedding. Many things I think I remember turn out to be something I dreamed once. Is that unusual?"

I smiled. "Probably not, if you're talking about childhood events. But do you often find it difficult to distinguish between something you've dreamed and some actual event? Other than the childhood stuff, I mean."

She thought about that briefly before replying. "There have been some adult things that . . . well, maybe I just dreamed them."

"Since, uh . . . ?"

"Adult. The past few years."

"Since your twentieth birthday, say?"

"Since then, probably, yes."

"Does Carl use dream analysis?"

"Not a lot."

"Not in the strictly Freudian sense?"

"I think not, no."

"Does he use hypnosis, regression techniques, any of that?"

"Gosh, I—not with me."

"But he has been your analyst these past five years."

"I have never thought of myself as being 'in analysis.' We've been friends. He advises me, counsels me."

"But you don't lie on a couch and . . . "

"Well, a few times. But nothing heavy."

"Nothing heavy."

"That's right."

"Like . . . "

"I've never discussed sex with him."

"Sex is heavy?"

"It is for me."

"Since when?"

"Since forever."

"Since your awareness of sex. Going back to when?"

She was becoming impatient with me, fidgety. "I guess I have always been aware of it. I cannot remember a time when I was not aware of it."

I commented, "That's, uh, pretty heavy, yeah. Where'd you go to school?"

"Right here. Poppa insisted on private tutors. I have never attended a real school."

"Poppa is TJ? Or JQ?"

"JQ. TJ never seemed to know if I was dead or alive."

"You never mention your mother," I pointed out.

"I have very little reason to," she replied. "I saw very little of my mother. I believe that she was gone, not here, for most of my life. I believe—it seems that—I think she came back right after Poppa died."

God, it was getting heavier and heavier.

I said, "Poppa died when you were thirteen. Then your mother and father less than a year later. Terry and Marcia took over your guardianship?"

"Yes."

"But you continued to have private tutors instead of going to regular school?"

"That's right."

"Did you like that?"

"I guess I never thought about it."

"You never questioned it, never rebelled, never thought how nice it would be to have people your own—"

She shut me down right there, coldly, finally. "I said I never thought about it. I have to start getting ready for dinner." She rose from the couch, gave me a frosty look. "See you later."

And that was it.

There was no doubt that the interview had ended.

The only question in my mind was who had ended it. I don't know who that lady was, the stiffly formal one with the frosty look.

I just knew that it was not Karen Highland.

CHAPTER EIGHT
From the Stream

I did not have time to fully assimilate the perplexing developments with Karen because another problem was awaiting me in my room—in the person of Marcia Kalinsky.

She was wearing a mini version of the terry cloth robe that was assuming proportions as uniform of the day in this household—and when I say "mini" I mean hip-length and obviously designed to enhance rather than conceal the feminine charms of the wearer. I have already noted on these pages the fact that Marcia was remarkably preserved and no slouch whatever in the feminine charms department—but I must add here that the casually belted minirobe, worn over nothing more than the bottom half of a skimpy bikini bathing suit, added nothing but strain to an already overstrained day.

I left the door wide open.

She closed it.

I kept on my feet and moving, trying to maintain a safe distance between polarized bodies.

She kept moving, also, continually closing that distance.

This was the mode of physical action during the ensuing conversation.

She: "Where the hell have you been? I've been waiting for damned near thirty minutes."

Me: "Sorry, I didn't know. I would have rushed right back. Uh, did we have an appointment?"

She: "Don't get cute. This is no time for cute. I want to know where you've been."

Me: "Not that it is any of your business, but purely because I have nothing to conceal, I have been with my client. Karen is my client. She is the sole reason—"

She: "Everything that goes on in this house is my business. Karen is my business. That girl is sick. Sick, sick. She's just so much raw meat for bastards like you. I want you out of here. And damned quick."

Me: "There seems to be a conflict here. Your husband has ordered me to stay for dinner. And I have been retained by the lady of the—"

She, furiously: "That bastard! Can't you see what he's doing? He's setting you up, asshole! Setting you up!"

I got back to the door and opened it, pointedly. "Let's continue this at dinner."

She hit the door with a straight arm to send it banging shut again. "We'll continue it right here! Did Terry offer you a contract?"

I was getting steamed. I went to the bar, found and lit a cigarette, only then noticed the half-empty fifth of Jim Beam and equally half-empty tumbler of booze-rocks. Hers, no doubt. The lady was deep into the cups, which perhaps explained her behavior.

I turned to her with a new try at patience only to find her pelvis riding my hip, and the balance of the conversation took place in that attitude.

Me: "You're right. It's no time for cute. Terry did not offer me a contract, no, he conferred one upon me. I gather it is the same type of indentured service conferred upon everyone who stumbles into this spiderweb. I'll bet that you are under a marital contract with identical provisions. How much free and clear per day are you getting, Marcia?"

She: "Not nearly enough. But that is all going to come tumbling down next week, so don't lose any sleep over it. I still want you out of here."

Me: "Not nearly as much as I want me out of here, lady. So don't you lose any sleep over that. Why will it tumble down?"

She: "The ride is over, that's all, the end is here. And I say thank God to that. But I'll still scratch your eyes out if you try moving in on that girl."

Me: "Look again, Marcia, that girl is no longer a girl. She's a bona fide woman, certifiably so, with a right to choose her own company. But if your concern is real, then that makes us allies, sort of. What sort of sick is she?"

She: "The sort of sick that makes her a natural for con men like you. Sick between the thighs, or hadn't you noticed, and don't try to say you haven't."

Me: "What you call sick others would call a basic human need—or don't you have those kinds of needs too?"

She: "Sure I have that kind of need. So what are you—a superjock? Big lover? Think you can handle eight to ten tussles a day?"

Me: "Do it right the first time, Marcia, who needs the other seven to nine?"

She: "I don't know. When do you want to show me?"

Me: "Well, there probably would not be time before dinner."

She: "Keep your dance card open, lover. Meet you back here at ten."

She snared her drink and headed for the door, opened it, turned back to say, "I can hardly wait."

I asked her, at that distance, "What is he setting me up for, Marcia?"

She giggled, waved the drink at me, and replied in departure, "Tell you at ten."

It would have been a great seduction routine if she had been wearing leather and dragging a whip—and certainly there had been an element of seduction to that entire encounter—but I had to vote for it as only a secondary motive for that visit to my bedroom.

The whole thing was beginning to spin around in my head, but without any clear vortex. Oh, sure, you are way ahead of me and thinking how obvious it ought to be by now. There have been forty thousand B-movies and God only knows how many television melodramas built around identical situations. We all must surely know, at this point, that Kalinsky has been looting the estate and milking the trusts for all they are worth and that, with Karen about to come into her own, she is probably also coming into mortal danger.

But I was immersed in a real-life situation and I have discovered that real life is not as malleable as fiction.

No one is that much in charge here. There's no script to follow and no director shouting instructions to a cast that is willing to blindly follow. Real life is not scripted, it is usually played by ear, and few of us ever know exactly why we do what we do or say what we say.

Fiction is economical, has to be, everything pointed toward a desired effect. Real life is luxurious, no matter what your station; the options are endless and occurring moment by moment, and very damned few things in the individual lifestream seem pointed toward anything in particular.

I cannot approach real life with fictional devices and neither can you.

So bear with me, here, and do not leap ahead to a synthetic conclusion. I could not afford to, even though everything inside of me was yelling at me to get the hell out.

What was the real reason behind Marcia's visit?

Was she really concerned for Karen or was that just a smoke screen—and, if a smoke screen, why would she feel it important to lay one around me?

Did she let it slip that big changes were arriving in the coming week, or had it been her intention all along to drop that information on me?

Had she really been trying to drive me away—or

had she merely been manipulating me into a challenge to stay?

What was the personal relationship with her husband—and was the sexplay just another smoke screen of some type, or was she really all that contemptuous of her marriage?

What, exactly, was "sick" about Karen—and, to whatever extent she may be so, how much of that was being deliberately engineered into her by this very strange household?

Why had a shrink been brought aboard? Out of genuine concern for an ailing heiress?—or as part of an elaborate plan to certify her as mentally incompetent and thus forestall a turnover of power?

And, if I could take Marcia at face value, exactly what was I being "set up" for?

I haul all of this out for inspection here so that you may consider the same puzzles that I had to consider at that moment and so that you may understand the frame of my mind while I was getting into a tuxedo that had been tailored for me during the hour or so before that moment, upon the orders of a man whom I had first met maybe two hours earlier and who, ironically enough, was married to a lady who had just metaphorically invited me to screw her brains out immediately after dinner.

I also give it to you here lest it all be lost sight of in the rapidly cascading developments of that evening at the Highland estate.

It was only about twenty minutes past seven, but I dressed early to check the fit. I was standing at the mirror inspecting same when I suddenly became aware of eyes upon me. My gaze went straight to the French doors. The sun had set and the balcony outside was cloaked in deep shadows, but I saw her as clearly as if she had been dipped in luminous paint.

It was Karen's ethereal companion and the expression on that tormented face was clearly pleading with me for something.

The apparition turned, showing itself in clear three-dimensional profile, to gaze down upon the patio, back to me, then once again onto the patio, as though summoning my attention to something there.

I did not give it a second thought nor a moment's hesitation but moved quickly to the balcony. The apparition had winked out with my first step forward, but I could still sense presence out there.

That particular presence, however, was not now the focus of my attention.

The focus was immediately below. Two men stood at the patio bar in twilight, a woman in an evening dress was walking toward the pool—and in the pool, submerged in deep water, a nude female figure floated facedown.

There are moments in the stream when the thinking mind stands aside and something deeply human yet more than human takes over the motor nerves to send a living creature sprawling into personal peril with no thought whatever for the self. I believe that such moments explain those singular, selfless acts of human heroism.

Of course I was thinking no such thoughts at that moment, and I am laying no claim to heroism. Quite the reverse, I am merely explaining a really stupid action. I have never been big on watersports, naval experience notwithstanding, and had never shown any particular form as a diver. I do not recall gauging the distance or extrapolating angle for depth; I remember only pushing with all the leg I had against the railing of that second-story balcony and launching myself headlong toward that floating body, the initial shock of penetration and a weird wandering apology to God knows who for immersing the tux, then the warm-cold naked flesh of Marcia Kalinsky as I fought the limp form toward a living environment.

CHAPTER NINE
Mirror Image

A woman was screaming and the patio area was filling rapidly with excited people in formal attire.

The guys in dinner jackets were standing by at poolside with hands outstretched to offer help at a distance and a third, whom I recognized a moment later as one who had been stocking the inside bar when I went through earlier that day, jumped in with more direct assistance. He groaned, "Oh no, it's Mrs. Kalinsky," as we hoisted her onto the deck.

The guy just stood there, fully clothed in waist-deep water, and watched with horror as I pulled myself out and went to work on the victim.

Someone brought a stack of towels and someone else yelled, "Get Powell—get the doctor!"

I had cleared Marcia's throat and produced a gush of water from the air tract when I became aware of the arrival of Kalinsky on the scene. I guess I half expected the guy to start moving among the guests and reassuring them because I was really surprised by his reaction. He came totally unglued, trying to get into the action and fighting me for position on the body.

I growled, "Cool it, Terry, she's okay!"

Someone wrestled him away, but still he lay there beside her, stroking her forehead while she coughed and gasped into the resurrection.

Carl Powell made the scene then, and smoothly took over. I was impressed by the guy's professionalism and situation management. He had her blanketed and stretchered and moving away from there before I could get my breathing under control.

Someone handed me a lighted cigarette and someone else put a glass of whiskey in my hand. There was a lot of crowding around and congratulating and slaps on the back, and I overheard one awed voice exclaim, "Yeah, they say he dove off of that balcony over there!"

I looked, myself, at the balcony under discussion and shuddered at the height and distance.

It was at about that moment that I became aware of a pain in the leg and a burning sensation inside the sodden dinner jacket. The tux was a disaster, split and scraped at several points; it was then I realized that I hadn't gotten off quite as cleanly as I'd thought. A finger was beginning to throb like hell and a warmth inside the trouser leg told me I was oozing blood somewhere.

Then Karen appeared, calmly beautiful in a chiffon-and-lace dinner gown. She took my hand without a word and led me through the crowd and into the house and up the stairs to her apartment, quietly and carefully undressed me to the skin and toweled me dry, applied stinging antiseptics to what turned out to be minor scrapes—apparently I had either touched bottom or grazed the side of the pool as I went in—then she put me to bed, pulled the sheet up over my chest, gently kissed me on the lips, and went away.

Without a single word between us, all that.

But, at the risk of sounding nerdy, words had not been necessary. Some sort of nonverbal communication had been passing between us all that while—from which I received sympathy, gratitude, admiration, concern, love—all of that.

I had felt neither the need nor the desire to resist the sweet ministrations. Actually, I felt like hell. There had been damned little sleep the night before, the day had begun early and with a bang, and it had been constant stress without letup ever since. I had eaten, during the preceding twenty-four hours or so, a raisin Danish and two cold chicken legs, and I guess I had used all the steam I had left on that twilight dunk in the Highland pool.

So I am not overly ashamed to admit that I simply let it all go and went to sleep in Karen's bed. I learned later that she had gone below and rescued the dinner party—which may seem a bit cold-blooded but, what the hell, that's the way things are done in high society—the show must go on, and all that.

Besides which, Marcia was apparently none too much the worse for her misadventure. She was "doing fine" and "resting comfortably," or so I was advised by Carl Powell when he roused me from my nap at about nine-thirty.

"You undoubtedly saved her life, though, you know," he told me soberly. "It was a real stroke of luck that you spotted her from your window. The lights had not been turned on yet in the pool area, so fifty people could have been standing around down there and never noticed her. Actually I understand that several guests were on the patio and thought it was just some kind of stunt when you came sailing overhead fully clothed. That was a hell of a nervy thing to do, I have to tell you."

He was inspecting my hurts during that little monologue.

"Damned lucky, I'd say, that this is all you got out of it. One inch less stretch and you would have ended up a leaky bag of bones at poolside."

I winced at that analogy, but let it pass without comment.

He flipped the sheet back over me and repeated, "Damned lucky."

I asked him, "Are you finished?"

He sighed as he replied, "Yeah. Just wanted to check you out, firsthand. Don't get much chance to play doctor around here, you know."

I sat up and reached for the cigarette he was then lighting. He passed it over and lit another for himself. I said, "Thought doctors are against smoking."

"Sure we are," he replied. "Damned things will kill you. But then so will sex, booze, airplanes and automobiles, and just plain food if you eat too much. Actually we start dying at conception. It would be just as valid to describe living as controlled dying. It's always in process."

"Matter of spatial relationships," I suggested.

"More or less," he agreed.

I asked, "Why was Marcia in the pool? I saw her at about a quarter after seven, at which time she had not yet dressed for dinner. Thought that's where she was headed when she left me."

He said, "Too much to drink, no doubt. Happens every week. Probably wanted to take a little dip and sober up. Guess she just passed out in the pool."

I reminded him, "She was naked."

He informed me, "Nothing unusual about that. Soon as the sun goes down . . . Marcia prefers nature in the raw."

I said, "She was wearing half a bikini and a hip-length robe when I saw her earlier."

"Yes. We found them in a chair on the patio. Also the dregs of pure whiskey in the bottom of a water glass."

I made a guilty face and told him, "It was still half full when she carried it away from my room. And a fifth of Jim Beam was half empty."

He asked, casually, "Did you two get it on?"

I replied, "Not at all. She was in my face over Karen. Called me a bastard and a con man, ordered me out of the house."

Powell grinned. "Well, that's Marcia."

I asked, casually, "What is Karen?"

The grin faded. He took a thoughtful pull at his cigarette and told me, "I studied your portfolio quite thoroughly, you know. I recommended your contract. You should accept it. I feel that you can be very helpful with Karen, maybe decisively so, lord knows more helpful than I have been."

I grunted.

He continued without pause: "I like your background, Ash. Nicely rounded, and you've gone into areas I've only recently begun to think about. I believe that could be Karen's out, perhaps her only out."

"Out of what?" I wanted to know.

He ignored my curiosity. "Indirectly, at least, I suppose I'm responsible for you two getting together in the first place. I sent her to Zodiac."

That one surprised me. I told him so.

He ignored that too, went on to say: "Reality can be very elusive any time you try to pin it down. I have spent the past twenty-two years studying the mind and, hell, I still usually feel like a blind man trying to lead the blind."

The guy was reaching me. I found myself wondering more about him than about my client. I asked him, "Is that why you sold your soul to the Highlands?"

The grin came back as he inspected that query. "Don't make the mistake of thinking that your soul is an island, Ash. It's as much a part of the continent as your body is. It is immune to being bought and sold because the original owner will not release the title."

Well, anyway, that was an alternate point of view to the one offered by Kalinsky. Or was it?

I said, "Which original owner is that?"

He said, "Good and evil are mere states of mind, aren't they? I know I don't have to tell you that because I know where you've been, but just so you'll understand that we are more or less on the same wavelength. They are simply alternate views of the same reality."

"We live in an asymmetrical universe," I pointed out, testing him.

"Ah yes," he replied instantly, "but it was pure symmetry before the bang."

I thought, bingo, but said aloud, "Which side of the mirror image do you suppose we inhabit?"

"Does it really matter?"

I replied, "Maybe not."

"Suppose for the sake of argument," he said soberly, "that both God and Satan do indeed exist, co-equals, each ruling his own half of the image. We, you and me, do not know which side of reality we inhabit. Do we not run a hell of a risk, then, in choosing sides?"

I grinned and told him, "You are suggesting, then, that we do have that choice."

"Quite the opposite. This is for the sake of argument, remember. God or Satan, whichever rules here, is a cosmic force with absolute power. If God is on our side, as we are constantly being implored to believe—which means, in the same sense, that we inhabit God's side of reality—then how can Satan manifest power here? And if Satan does not manifest power in our reality, then where do we get all the agony, all the greed, all the brutality?"

I suggested, "Reason from the other end—start with agony, greed, brutality, and tell me which reality that describes. Sounds to me, in that argument, like we came down on the wrong side."

He said, "Exactly."

I said, "But maybe asymmetry is purely a mathematical concept, and maybe our math models have the same limitations as the dimensioned minds that fashion them. Maybe we have asymmetrical minds, Carl. Could we ever then see true symmetry—and would we even recognize it if we did?"

He slapped his leg and said, "Jesus! You've struck a nerve!"

I suggested, "We all are a bit premature in handing down judgments on cosmic questions. We can't even find cosmos, can we? So how the hell do we circumscribe it?"

"Exactly!"

I said, "What kind of sick is Karen?"

He replied, "Dreadfully."

I pointed out, "If I am going to help . . . "

He got up and left the room, returned a minute later with a bottle and two glasses, sloshed some whiskey into each and handed me one, belted his, wiped his lips with the back of his hand, said, "It's a violation of ethics, but I am going to regard this as a consultation, so I'm holding you to confidentiality too."

I said, "Okay," and belted mine.

He refilled the glasses, peered into his, said, "She has an unresolved sexual conflict."

I said, "Tell me about it."

"Electra complex. Well . . . I don't really buy Freud's whole bag of tricks, especially not as they would apply to the general population, but I guess that is the basic Freudian weakness; he tried to extend clinical psychology—that is, mental pathology, into an explanation of the whole psychogenetic and sociopathic structure of mankind. As much as to say that the diseased mind presents a valid diagram of mankind in general. I don't buy that, never did. But Freud was a genius, let's not sell him short. And Karen's personality profile fits perfectly into the Freudian complex characterized by an unnatural love for her father."

I said, "But Freud himself did not buy the Electra complex."

"Touché," replied the good doctor, "but it does not change anything. Freud did elaborate the Oedipus complex, which is simply the reverse case. I have always found that the sauce for the goose is equal sauce for the gander. But if you want to get picky, call Karen's sauce an Oedipus complex and I won't get mad at you. Point is, there is this unresolved conflict that is simply eating her alive."

"Would you consider it characteristic, then," I mused, "that she now claims to have very little feeling for either parent?"

"If not characteristic," he replied, "then certainly not destructive to the theory. Such complexes are caused by feelings prisoner to the subconscious realm. That is where they do their dirt. She could consciously hate her father while still gripped by the guilt generated within the subconscious."

"You see it as a guilt trip, then."

"That is the destructively moving force, yes. And,

of course, in this case compounded by feelings of guilt over the untimely death of both parents."

"Why would she feel guilt over that?"

"Because," he replied, pausing to belt the second shot, "she thinks she killed them."

I said, dumbly, "What?"

"Thinks she put a bomb on their boat. TJ had been in bed, sick with the flu. Elena had already made plans to take the boat out that day. TJ began feeling better and joined her at the last minute. Karen backed out at the last minute, tried her best to keep TJ home too. The boat exploded in flames forty feet out of the slip. Karen thinks she did it."

I said, "Shit." Then I belted my second and added, "So what do you think?"

"I think," said my new drinking buddy, the mystic shrink, "that it is all very tragic."

Enter, now, our mutual good buddy and keeper of souls, Terry Kalinsky. He is in a hell of a dither.

"Thank God I found you guys here!" he yelled. "We got a hell of a problem!"

Powell placed the bottle on the floor beside the bed and surged to his feet. "Is she . . . ?"

"Naw, shit, it's Karen again! She came in to see how Marcia was doing and Marcia flipped out, said all kinds of crazy shit. Karen ran out into the god-damn night and is right now wandering around the neighborhood somewhere all alone in the damned dark. I sent all the men out looking for her—very quietly, we don't want the guests in on this and . . ."

Powell was already moving toward the door. I was staggering around trying to find some clothing.

" . . . I'm just hoping you guys have some idea where she may have gone. Jesus Christ, it's pitch dark out there and that kid—"

I grabbed him by the chin to shut him up. "What did Marcia say to her?"

"Aw, some crazy shit about—said Karen tried to kill her, said she saw Karen watching her as she dived into the pool—crazy, it's crazy!"

"How did Karen try to kill her, Terry?"

He laughed, almost hysterically. "By psychic force, I guess, if you want to believe that shit. Marcia said Karen held her under by psychic force. Can you believe that shit?"

I could, yes.

I could believe that shit.

CHAPTER TEN
Maxim

Is it possible to kill with the mind? It has never been done, to my knowledge, under laboratory conditions—nor have I heard of anyone in modern times being hauled into court charged with psychic murder or manslaughter—but the literature of mankind, including holy writ, is rich with examples of human preoccupation with just that sort of power.

Consider, if you will, the witch scare of early America—which, at its height, was but an extreme realization of a centuries-old terror exported to the New World from England. Consider also the voodoo priests who rule certain religious convictions of the Caribbean area, also ages old and imported from Africa.

I toss these two up as ready examples for easy recognition by almost any literate person, but there are thousands more, and they have their roots in virtually every culture on the planet.

Of course such preoccupations today are instantly labeled, by those in the know, as superstitious claptrap. And maybe they are. We do not have to look much farther than our television sets to realize that a leading human trait is suggestibility, and that there are always those among us who will seek to exploit that trait to their own advantage. That could well be the real story behind today's shamans, witches, and other black magicians, as well as religionists of various hues.

But a pure scholar or scientist will want to know a lot more than the evidence available today is able to tell us about the origins of ideas in the human belief system. We may, as a species, be naturally suggestible or gullible—but what made us that way?

Can a shaman wield power over any individual who has no living or genetic memory of an actual "supernatural" event? And for a modern definition of *supernatural*, we have only to look at the so-called Cargo Cults of New Guinea, born during World War II among primitive tribesmen who could not make the natural link between cause and effect with respect to their "manna from heaven" dropped from American cargo planes.

To this very day the shamans of New Guinea continue to build crude mock-ups of aircraft upon mountaintops to attract the pleasure of gods long departed from their skies, and they may well go on doing so for centuries out of mind if their culture remains isolated from the tide of human evolution. So somewhere about the year 2550, descendants of the World War II shamans may begin to question this superstitious practice, pointing out that no gods have been seen in the skies over New Guinea in living memory and therefore probably never were—so who the hell do these guys think they're kidding?

I do not know how pure I may be as scholar or scientist, but I do not close the door on witches or shamans or any others without wanting to know a hell of a lot more than I can know about the heart of their belief systems.

How did the witch idea get started? Did someone see or experience something so mind-blowing as to anchor a possibility within human psyche for generations to come?—and have others added fuel to that possibility by duplicating, at least to some extent, that experience?

Or how many "superstitions"—examined and fully understood by the modern mind—would fall neatly into "natural" but "real" categories, as easily and accurately explainable as the cargo gods?

Is it possible to kill with the mind? Millions upon millions of modern humans believe it possible to heal with the mind and to sicken with the mind. The entire science of psychosomatic medicine is built upon that belief. And how many medical doctors with no interest whatever in psychosomatic or psychic/religious phenomena have consigned a medical prognosis to the patient's own "will to live"?

Is it possible, then, to fabricate a thesis that may explain a purely psychic power that can and does manipulate matter? I think so. I have been toying with one for years. And I need no supernatural laboratory in which to examine it. It is, actually, implicit in virtually every discovery of science during the Age of Einstein. So I find my anchor not in superstition and black magic but in the basic modern tenets of physical science.

Is it possible to kill and/or to otherwise manipulate matter with the mind? I say yes, with the shamans; yes, with the witches; yes, with Jesus and Gautama and all the mystics; yes, with Einstein and Bohr and Planck; yes, with modern medicine.

The full exposition of my thesis would fill a book of its own, so I give you here only the maxims from which it operates:

> Pure energy is the underlying reality of the space-time continuum; in its purest form, energy is never more than wave-potential.
>
> The potential of energy manifests as matter imbedded within structured energy fields that themselves result from fluctuations within the energy constant.
>
> Consciousness is an energy constant, expressing as wave-potential.
>
> Self-consciousness, or Knowingness, is a fluctuation within a consciousness continuum.
>
> Fluctuation within a consciousness field may be produced by "thought" and/or may be expressed as "thought" inside space-time.
>
> Since fluctuations within the energy constant are the source of all "matter" and since consciousness itself is an energy constant influenced by thought, it therefore holds that thoughts may produce matter and may be said to be capable of physically influencing matter.

ASHES TO ASHES

Is it possible to kill with the mind? Do not ever bet your life that it is not.

CHAPTER ELEVEN
Rendezvous

"When you think of LA, think of a nation." Someone once said that in print, I don't remember who, but the reference was to life-style, multiplicity of cultures and industries, the human equation.

When I think of LA, I think of a county, because it is literally impossible to separate the city proper from the sprawl of neighboring communities that crowd the coastal plain from the San Gabriel Mountains to the Pacific—and, actually, I guess I think of two counties, because Disneyland and Knotts Berry Farm and the charming beach communities of the south coast are in Orange County—well, really, four, five, or six counties when you start trying to make the cut, because you have to also include parts of San Bernardino, Riverside, San Diego, and Ventura counties to really think LA.

But if you just consider LA County by itself, we are talking more than seventy-five incorporated cities encompassing some four thousand square miles and a population that exceeds that of more than forty of our states, seventy-five miles of coastline, nine hundred square miles of desert. Forget all the bad press and one-line jokes, it's the most interesting big city in the world; smog and freeway jams are a small enough price to pay for the privilege of calling this area home. But I guess it's the geographical contrasts that I like best: mountains, valleys, canyons, beaches, deserts, all intermingled like disparate pieces of a jigsaw puzzle yet so harmoniously blended into urban/suburban environments.

I give you this not as a hype to immigration (one of the more common bumper stickers lately seen on local freeways reads: Welcome to California—Now Go Home), but to relate you properly to the scene of Karen Highland's disappearance.

If you have been thinking of Bel Air as a typical urban neighborhood but just a bit richer than most, then you cannot really visualize the problem. Bel Air is a jumble of hills and canyons, twisting roads and near-vertical lanes and driveways set into the Santa Monica Mountains. Leave one of the main drives, of which there are very few, and you are in a maze of rambling, twisting, plunging, sometimes corkscrewing country lanes with no apparent logic and often no obvious way out.

It can be trying enough feeling your way through Bel Air in broad daylight and with a neighborhood map; try it on a moonless night with the wind beginning to whip a bit and scudding clouds cloaking the hilltops and misting the roadways.

Yet Beverly Hills is a stone's throw east, UCLA and Westwood just across Sunset Boulevard to the south, the San Fernando Valley with its million-plus population over the hills to the north. Due west is absolutely zilch, though—nowhere, nothingness, the great spine of the Santa Monicas—wilderness.

Kalinsky was understandably upset. A person could disappear into that nighttime environment and never be seen again except as a pile of bleached bones accidentally discovered months or years later by a backpacker.

I was upset, too, primarily because of the questionable emotional state of my client. But there are crazies in the land, too, and no one likes to think of any woman wandering around alone in the night in any part of LA.

I had no idea whatever as to where the other searchers were looking, how many were looking, or if there was any particular logic to the search. Apparently Kalinsky was remaining on the premises, both to anchor the party, which was still in progress, by now loudly so and centered around the lounge off the patio, and to serve as headquarters contact for the search operation.

I later learned that the security force numbered a dozen men and that they were in constant radio communication with each other, so I assume in hindsight that some concerted plan of action was in place.

I didn't know about Doc Powell. He was off and running even before I cleared Karen's apartment, which I abandoned wrapped in a towel. By the time I got to my room and into my own clothing, he had a good five-minute jump on me.

So, as I said, I didn't know what the hell was really

happening around me. I went straight to the Maserati, liberated a Walther PPK 9mm pistol, which I customarily store in a trick floorboard compartment and which I now placed on the seat beside me, and went cruising with no particular route in mind.

Don't ask why I wanted the gun. It was a dark, misty night and I was in alien territory seeking a needle in a haystack; maybe the Walther gave me a feeling of power, a refutation of the impotence creeping through me.

I was worried, yes. But I tried to focus the emotion and put it to work for me, maybe to highlight and sensitize some vaguely realized aspect of consciousness—or, to put it in popular lingo, I was "going for vibes."

Trouble with that is, you seldom know which "vibes" to trust. I cruised aimlessly along Bellagio Drive for a couple of wasted minutes, then just gave the Maserati her head. Almost instantly she did a U-turn in a broad driveway and went back past the Highland estate and onto Stone Canyon Road.

But hell, it was pitch black out there, the headlights forming a well-defined cone extending into mistville. The compass was showing a heading of generally north with an occasional swing to NNW. I had gone several minutes past any lighted structures when suddenly we veered up a little lane and, seconds after that, into a dead end.

I sat there for a moment, wondering just what the hell had brought me there, then I got out and walked around the car a couple of times before venturing on.

I was in the wilds, pal, pure wilds, and in a stygian,

vapory darkness that hungrily swallowed the pathetic little beam from my pencil-flash. But I had found a trail, and it seemed to be curving gently upward along one of the many canyons that characterize the topography of that area.

I paused a couple of times to wonder if I was nuts or what to be out there staggering about the darkened countryside—this, to show you how fine and uncertain the extrasensory influence can be—and wondering how much more rope I was willing to give this particular vibration.

But then I had a rush and a wild chill tickling my spine, and I knew that I was on target.

I found her a moment later, crumpled across the trail, weeping like a lost child, something wet and sticky and odorous soaking the chiffon dress.

I found the doc, too, in her arms, his head bashed in and obviously all the life bashed out of him.

No psychic killing, that one.

It stunned me, I mean really stunned me in all the fine ramifications of the event.

I have told you that I was no more than five minutes behind Powell, then I had wandered for maybe another two or three minutes before finally homing-in on this very spot with no dallying along the way—but there had been the sensation, at least, of covering quite a bit of ground in a vehicle during that brief travel.

So where the hell was I?—and how the hell had Powell gotten here so fast?—for that matter, how the hell had Karen gotten here so quickly, on foot?—and how the hell had Powell known exactly where to find her for this rendezvous with death?

Besides which, I felt such an overpowering sadness over the death of this man with whom I had felt so close in such a short time.

And I had this equally overpowering sense of sadness for Karen and the terrible goddamn mess her life seemed to have fallen into.

I felt for life signs, even though I knew there would be none. The whole front of his skull was crushed in and blood was everywhere.

All the while Karen was rocking him in her arms and sobbing over and over, "I'm sorry, I'm so sorry . . . "

It took me a while to pry her loose and disentangle her from the still-warm corpse and get her onto her feet, then I half carried, half led her back along the trail and put her into the car.

Then I put myself in and cranked up the mobile phone and called the cops. I did not know exactly where I was, but I gave the location as best I could and told the dispatcher I'd leave my headlights on.

Next I called Kalinsky, briefed him, suggested he call his lawyer, and hung up on his spluttering.

Then I lit a cigarette and settled in for the wait. Karen was into a blank stare. She had not uttered a word except for the automatic speech noted above.

It took about ten minutes for the police response. An LAPD black-and-white rolled up as I was finishing a second cigarette. I had not thought of the Walther again until that very moment, but decided then and there to slip it onto the floor and kicked it under the seat as I got out to meet the cops.

Two other cars came screeching in before the cops hit the ground.

Kalinsky and troops.

It was going to be a long night.

It was, indeed, a very long night.

CHAPTER TWELVE
Time Factor

The suspected "weapon" turns out to be a rock weighing about ten pounds, roughly the size and shape of a football. Theory has it that Karen could easily heft such a stone in both hands, raise it overhead, and smash it against a human skull with sufficient force to crush same.

Another theory has Karen alone and terrified in the night, mistaking Powell for an attacker and thus putting his lights out.

This without benefit of any input whatever from Karen, herself. She is seated in my car, staring blankly at nothing, while a guy introducing himself as MacIlliney or MacAllaney, the staff lawyer, holds her hand in silence. He is no more than thirty years old and very ill at ease in the situation.

There are other people all over the damned place. There are also floodlights, helicopters, ambulances, many police units, couple of television crews with minicams getting no cooperation whatever from the officials.

Some of Kalinsky's people are quietly discussing fine points of the law with some plainclothes cops.

Kalinsky himself is pacing nervously about, obviously awaiting the arrival of something or someone else, shooting me an occasional murderous glance and muttering under his breath.

I am leaning against the front fender of the Maserati, arms crossed, feeling almost like a casual spectator until a uniformed cop approaches with a clipboard and asks me to sign my statement. I scan it and sign it, hand the clipboard back, the cop thanks me politely and walks away.

The night wears on.

The cops seem bent on an interview with Karen over the continued objections of Kalinsky's people. There seems to be a standoff of sorts.

Finally, Kalinsky's "someone" arrives in a chauffered limousine. Kalinsky runs over and climbs inside; I get a glimpse of a silver-haired man wearing a business suit.

It is midnight, now.

The cops have completed "securing the scene." The corpse has been transported. There has been a huddle around an open door of the limousine. Kalinsky emerges from the huddle, goes to my car, takes Karen and the lawyer to the limousine. I follow, because I am the curious type.

I hear a plainclothes cop refer to the man in the limousine as "your honor." Another guy in the huddle is apparently representing the DA's office. There is some give and take, there, outside the limousine, before Karen is allowed to enter. Fine points of law again. Or, maybe, fine points of bending the law. I overhear phrases such as "medical affidavits" and "conservator's certification" and I begin to get the drift.

A "conservator" is someone appointed by a court to manage the affairs of a mental incompetent.

Through all of this, Karen stands woodenly with head bowed. As she is being helped into the limousine, though, she swivels her head to stare directly at me. Our eyes clash for maybe a tenth of a second and then she is inside and the car is moving. I am left with an electric jolt racing through my nerve tissue and I know that she knows what is happening to her.

One of Kalinsky's men comes over to me, a guy I now know as Herbert, to give me an edge on the flow.

"She will be booked on a preliminary charge of simple manslaughter and immediately released to Mr. Kalinsky's custody."

I said, "That's nice."

"Mr. Kalinsky will be wanting a conversation with you immediately upon his return from the police station."

I said, "That's fine."

"You are to make no further statements to the police or to the press unless Mr. Kalinsky is present."

I said, "That's right."

But as soon as Herbert spun on a military toe and marched away, I ambled over to the DA's man and told him, "She didn't do it, you know."

He smiled at me and said, "You are . . . ?"

I smiled back as I replied, "I are the guy who

found them out here, your principal material witness."

"Mr. Ford."

"That's right. And apparently I found them too quick. There is a time problem. It was a cute trick, but not quite cute enough. Do you know what is at stake here?"

The guy went right on smiling as he told me, "Yes, I do, Mr. Ford. I would say that my entire political career is at stake here."

I said, "Too bad," and left the guy staring at my back as I went on to the Maserati and got the hell away from there.

I made a beeline to the Highland estate while jotting down distance traveled for every compass heading and trying to maintain a steady 30 mph pace. It took me just under three minutes to hit the front gate, which figures about a mile and a half of distance traveled via the most direct roadways.

The gate guard had nothing to tell me about traffic through there before midnight since his shift had begun at that time.

I put the Maserati in the same parking space as before, but she was now the only vehicle in the area. Obviously the party was over. I retrieved the Walther and tucked it inside the waistband of my shorts, then went on toward the pool.

The service force was busily restoring order to the patio-lounge area. The bartender who helped me with Marcia was cleaning the island bar outside; he looked up at my approach and recognized me with a smile so I steered that way and went over to thank him for the assist, then I asked him in a casual way when he had last seen Miss Highland.

He replied that she had come into the lounge at "a bit" past nine o'clock, apparently while the dinner guests were dawdling over desserts, to check on the musicians and to make sure that all was in readiness there.

"You haven't seen her since then?" I asked.

He dropped his chin and leaned a bit closer in the response. "No sir, not since then, but something very strange has been going on around here the past couple of hours. I think maybe Miss Highland had another one of her spells or something. I mean, the whole executive staff is very uptight and they sent the guests home early."

I thanked him and started away, then checked myself and leaned back to inquire, very casually, "Mr. Kalinsky get back yet?"

The guy gave me a blank look and replied, "I wondered where he was, I mean I figured he was with Mrs. Kalinsky. Haven't seen him since, uh, since I guess right after Miss Highland."

"You mean since right after dinner."

"Yes sir, it—well, I guess more like about nine-thirty. He was looking for her—Miss Highland—asked me if she'd come through. Because by then the party had moved out here, you know, here on the patio and in the game room. Because people were dancing and—about nine-thirty, yes sir."

"He was in a dither," I suggested.

"Sure was."

I asked, "See Doc Powell around that same time?"

The guy was beginning to wonder about all these questions. He was getting an edge to the eyes and the body language was definitely one of withdrawal. "Not since we pulled Mrs. Kalinsky out of the pool, no sir."

I thanked him again and went on inside.

There was no sign of life whatever in the executive wing. The operations center was shut down and darkened except for a small nightlight at the back wall. I expected the executive office to be locked, as well, but the doors were not even closed, not even the one to the inner sanctum.

My unsigned contract still lay on the desk. There was evidence, also, that Kalinsky had quit the place in a hurry: an open cigarette humidor, a dead butt with an inch-long ash still attached in the ashtray, a doodle pad with several used sheets filled with hieroglyphics and detached, but not discarded; more importantly, a lighted LED on the telephone console indicating "Record Pause."

I studied the console for a moment, doped it, rewound the tape through three brief conversations, and hit the playback.

My own voice came through the speaker, bearing the message of my grisly find out Stone Canyon.

Then Kalinsky cussing in a husky voice to himself, then a dial-out followed by a brief and cryptic conversation:

"Yeah."

Kalinsky: "Okay, it's hit. Meet me out front in two minutes. Better bring the squad."

"Are we ready for this?"

"We better be. Where's Herb?"

"He's mobile."

"Okay, we'll catch him on the way. Better bring Mac."

"He's been partying. May not be ready."

Kalinsky: "Fuck that, just bring 'im."

A hang-up, another dial-out, but already I was beginning to sort the players. "Herb" was no doubt Herbert, one of the security honchos; "Mac" was MacIlliney or MacAllaney, the lawyer who had hand-held Karen during the ordeal in my car.

The second call-out was much more cryptic and even more brief:

"Yes, hello."

"This is TK. I need that package. Can you get started?"

The other voice was cultured, mature, maybe even silvery-haired. "You mean, right now? Do you know what time it is?"

"We both better know what time it is. Get started. I'll contact you on the mobile."

That was it. I removed the cassette and put it in my pocket, replaced it with a blank, then gathered up the doodles and took them, also, and got the hell out of there.

I wanted a moment with Marcia before Kalinsky and his goons returned to the palace.

And maybe, time allowing, a shot at Doc Powell's doodles.

Time allowing . . .

The time factor had become all-important. As important, probably, as life and death.

CHAPTER THIRTEEN
Engineering

The Kalinsky quarters seemed to be a mirror image of Karen's apartment, about the same size but reversed in layout, and upstairs over the executive offices.

Marcia was propped up with pillows on a large, overstuffed couch. She wore silk pajamas and a dressing gown but was otherwise uncovered. A large-screen projection TV was playing an old movie at murmuring volume. She seemed a bit pale but otherwise looked none the worse for the near-drowning experience.

I said, "How you doing?"

It was a different Marcia from the one I'd known as she replied, "Much better now, thanks. I understand you saved my life. Thanks."

I showed her a grin and a shrug. "Seemed the thing to do."

She said, "You're a nice man. And I have been a terrible jerk. Sorry."

I did not argue the point. I just said, "Sure."

"Have they found Karen?"

I said. "Yeah. She's going to be okay."

"Thank God. It was a stupid thing I—did you hear about that?"

I replied, "I heard a version. Like to hear yours."

"Why?"

I said, "Karen is in deep trouble. She came to me for help. I am trying to help. But I need a handle. What did you say to her?"

Her gaze fell away and there was a brief silence before she replied, "I'd had too much to drink, but I was not that drunk. I went down to make sure the staff was properly setting up for dinner. Then I thought I might as well take a quick dip because there really wasn't time for me to bathe and all. As I entered the pool, I saw Karen standing in the shadows by the diving board. She was wearing her yellow bikini. I remember thinking, well how 'bout that, she remembered her suit this time and she doesn't really need it. I mean, we always skinny-dip here after dark. I was looking for her as I came up, to see if she was coming in with me. I was looking straight at her and she was looking straight at me. I know our eyes were locked all during that horrible struggle."

I said, "What horrible struggle?"

"I could not get to the surface." She shivered in the memory of it. "It was as though a hand was holding me under and I could not escape it. I fought like the devil, let me tell you, but no matter what I did there was always a few inches of water above my head."

"How do you account for that?"

She shifted position slightly on the couch and gave me a flash with the eyes. "Come on, now. How would you account for it?"

I said, "I suppose you know my background."

She replied, "I sure do. And I'm sure you know what happened to me down there tonight."

I inquired, "Has Karen ever before, to your direct knowledge, exhibited any such power?"

She immediately replied, "Nothing I can put my finger on, no. I mean, nothing like that. But we've talked about it. You know, telekinesis, telepathy, psychic phenomena. I've had an interest in that stuff ever since Bridey Murphy. We've talked about it a lot. And lately Karen has seemed almost obsessed with it."

I said, "Has she spoken to you about her ethereal companion?"

"Her what?"

"A spirit, or something, that comes to her."

She said, "No, I have not heard of that."

I said. "Tell me about Elena."

"Elena. God. She's been dead ten years."

"Did you like her?"

"Never really knew her. Look, I know what happened to me tonight. It was dumb of me to yell at Karen that way, but I damn sure knew what I was yelling about. She tried to kill me."

"Why would she want to do that?"

"Beats the hell clear out of me. I'm the only real friend she has had all these years."

"But you never really knew Elena. Why not? She

was around for—what?—more than fifteen years before she died? And you were here, too, most of that time?"

She said, "I was here all the time, but Elena was not. Not much, anyway. Until that last year, and then—well, we just were not together all that much."

I said, "If Elena was not here then, where was she?"

"In institutions one after another, I guess."

"What sort of institutions?"

"You know what sort of institutions."

"What was her problem?"

Marcia sighed, as though suddenly becoming weary of the conversation. "I'd guess," she said quietly, "that JQ was her Number One problem."

"How so?"

She sighed again and replied, "Look, don't quote me on any of this. I don't know all of the facts and I doubt that anyone now living knows all the facts. But it seems that JQ never liked Elena. He was very upset by TJ's marriage, and I believe he just never accepted it. So he could not very well accept Elena, either, could he?"

"But he accepted Karen?"

"Absolutely doted on her. JQ's one soft spot was that kid. He spent the final two years of his life, while he knew he was dying of cancer, setting up his affairs so that most everything would go directly to Karen instead of to his own son."

I said, "That's interesting. And now she is about to come into all that. Is that what you had reference to when you told me, earlier tonight, that things here would be changing soon?"

She said, "I told you that?"

I said, "Words to that effect. You also told me that Terry was setting me up for something. We had a date for ten o'clock—remember?—when you were supposed to tell me what I was being set up for."

Marcia smiled a bit uncomfortably and said, "Give a girl a break, eh? I drink too much. And I am not very smart when I drink." She made a rueful face. "Well, what the hell—why not? No, I probably had something else in mind when I mentioned big changes. I'm leaving here next Saturday. And never looking back."

That last bit gave me pause. I said, "You mean . . . you are leaving Terry? Or you are both—?"

"You bet I am. Look, I was little more than a kid, myself, when I came here. Now I'm practically a middle-aged matron, and enough is enough. I made the commitment a long time ago to stick it out here with Karen and now the commitment is fulfilled. I'm leaving one week from tonight."

"Terry know about this?"

"No."

"Karen know about it?"

"No. That makes you my confidant, doesn't it? So please honor it. I'll tell them my own way, in my own time."

I said, "Sure."

She said, "Just you and Carl."

I said, "Carl knows?"

She replied, "He'd better. He's going with me."

I thought but did not say, "Oh shit." I did say, "You are not worried about Terry's reaction?"

"Of course we are worried about Terry's reaction. But there is nothing he can do to stop it, now."

I told her, very quietly, "You could be wrong about that, Marcia."

She saw it in my eyes, the emotion that I was trying to conceal. I had to break the eye contact. She squirmed about on the couch, removed a pillow, slowly transferred it to the floor, very quietly inquired, "Exactly what are you trying to tell me?"

I took her hand, squeezed it between both of mine, looked squarely into those worried eyes, and told her, "Carl is dead. Karen has been charged with his death."

She moaned, "Oh my God!"

I said, "Can you think of any reason why—?"

She cried, "Just get out of here! Please! Get out!"

I offered, "I'll shut up and just hang out for a while, if you'd like."

Tears had erupted and were bathing her cheeks. "No, just please . . . leave me alone."

I went out of there feeling like a bastard.

But Karen was the client, Marcia was not, and right then Karen needed all the help I could engineer for her.

I was giving it my best shot.

CHAPTER FOURTEEN
Contexts

Several things troubled me about that interview with Marcia. There were content problems and context problems. How much could I believe? Was there any reason for not believing all of it?

Putting the thing in context with our first two encounters, I had to first make allowance for the fact that the first two were colored by alcohol while the third was not only cold sober but also post-trauma.

And while two and possibly three moods or personality movements had been displayed during those interactions, at least one apparently dominant character trait came through in all three: forthrightness, a sort of natural honesty. There was a refreshing directness to that character, even when she was trying to be otherwise.

Even so, she had displayed an amazing candor in revealing her plan to run away with Carl Powell. I must tell you here, though—and I hope you can take the comment as clinical, without ego—that I have noted a tendency among women in general, who know about my background and interests, to be sometimes embarrassingly candid with me in highly personal matters, even some who are normally secretive and deceptive with others.

So much so, in fact, that I have had to recognize a certain intimidation factor inherent in the label of *psychic*—not nearly as much in men as in women, however—to the degree that I have learned not to discuss my work or "talents" in purely social contacts. I have found that women are generally more receptive than men to the reality of psychism—that is, more believing. I have an interesting theory to explain that, but I will not go into that here.

The point is that I am frequently told much more than I really want to know about a woman's interior life—as if to say, what the heck, he already knows it anyway so let's talk about it.

That factor could have been at work during that late-night conversation with Marcia Kalinsky.

I decided to accept—at least for the moment—the question of basic context and go on to the more troubling questions of content. And, really, a lot of bothersome stuff had been developed during that brief talk.

The most bothersome to me, vis-à-vis Karen Highland, was the information about her dead mother, Elena. A lot of powerfully operative stuff, there—operative, that is, upon the developing mind of a child—possibly traumatic stuff. No way could I miss the obvious, there: Was Elena the ethereal companion? If so, did she exist as an actual disembodied entity drawn to this plane by the frustrations of previous life here or did she exist purely as a traumatized spin-off from Karen's own troubled consciousness.

Bear with me, please. I am contextualizing content, here. This is important stuff, much too important to bang against a stone wall of preconceived notions.

Karen had given me to understand that she did not know the identity of this "visitor." She had also stated that the visits had begun in her early childhood, had grown more frequent in later years—and, I gathered, personally bothersome to Karen during recent times.

She claimed very little conscious memory associated with either parent, even though she was fourteen years old at the time of their deaths. She had also told me of a certain confusion in distinguishing dreams from actual events.

Could her memory of childhood visits, which she now likened to the ethereal visitations, actually be confused memories of actual physical events involving her actual mother during those infrequent periods when Elena was "between institutions?"—and was that now the source of a traumatically spun-off psychic-companion personality?

Her father, TJ, was—by the record—as much a recluse as his father, JQ, which means that he must have been under roof, so to speak, throughout Karen's early life. Why, then, did she exhibit such careless memory of her father?

Carl Powell, if I could believe my conversation with him, had her diagnosed as an Electra. In the

Electra complex, a female child is in love with her father and hates her mother as a competitor for the father's affection. If he had probed through her conscious and subconscious memories to that extent, could he have missed entirely the ethereal companion?"

Or had Carl Powell been as big a rat as Terry Kalinsky now seemed to be shaping into and had he merely helped to manufacture a psychopath—or an apparent psychopath—to help Kalinsky keep control of the Highland billions?

Was Karen Highland a psychopath or merely a victim of human greed?

Was she a killer?—and I had to take in, now, the question of her own parents, Bruno, perhaps even Bruno's brother—who thus far was only a postscript, but not a forgotten postscript, to this developing drama—Marcia's mishap in the pool, and of course Karen's psychiatrist and Marcia's imputed lover, Carl U. Powell, M.D.

It was a time for answers and all I had were questions.

And don't tell me to use my psychic powers. I do not use them, they use me.

But I would have gratefully accepted any small crumbs that they would feel inclined to toss my way.

Time was quickly running out for Karen Highland. And maybe for Ashton Ford. I had to find some answers, and I had to find them damned quick.

CHAPTER FIFTEEN
Resonating

Doc Powell's quarters were in the same wing as Karen's and were expansive enough to house also a small dispensary and a paneled study. I learned later that this had been JQ's apartment for his final two years, during which time he had confined himself within those walls. It had been a period of considerable discomfort and pain, which perhaps accounts for the depressing atmosphere I encountered there.

I have found that unhappy human experiences, especially those of a repetitive or continuous nature occurring within the same physical reference, or a singular event experienced with severely traumatizing emotions, somehow become imbedded in the molecular structures of that space-time field and sometimes never dissipate to the point where a sensitive person does not resonate them.

Sometimes the resonance is there long after the purely physical structure has been totally destroyed—so maybe the very earth, itself, is imbedded with this unhappiness.

To illustrate that latter connection, I remember an incident a few years ago when I was driving through one of the western states—Wyoming, maybe—and picked up a very strong emotional resonance while stopped at a rest area along the interstate highway. It was a feeling of desperation and despair mixed with terror. Casual questioning of a maintenance man brought out the story of a homesteading pioneer family of ten massacred on the site by an Indian war party. This some one hundred years earlier, yet somehow the event remained indelibly impressed in the space-time matrix despite the disappearance of all physical traces.

I was very uncomfortable in Powell's quarters, despite the fact that they were charmingly decorated and pleasing to the masculine sense of comfort. This feeling of discomfort had nothing to do with the knowledge that I was working on very short time before Kalinsky or the cops, or both, came looking for the same thing I was looking for.

I had that feeling of urgency, yes, but it was quite distinct and apart from some disturbingly resonating factor impressed within those walls. I did not know, at the time, that JQ had died in that apartment nor did I have any specific feeling as to the nature of the disturbance; I knew only that unhappiness had lived there.

This, coupled with the time-factor urgency, may have had some effect upon the efficiency of my search. I did find an entire library of open-reel tapes, indexed by date and covering psychoanalytic sessions with Karen over a five-year period. The periodicity indicated semiweekly sessions over the entire period, which seemed to make a liar out of Karen. She had told me point-blank that she had never thought of herself as being "in analysis."

The surface evidence seemed to indicate that she had been involved in some very heavy analysis. There were over five hundred such tapes, a fact that foreclosed any thought of carrying them away from there—besides which, it would have required probably a thousand hours to simply listen to that entire library, perhaps five thousand to come to any conclusions about the information that might be recorded there. I had no such time at my disposal. Five hours would have been regarded as a great luxury of time.

Of much greater value, in the given circumstances, would have been some sort of cross-index or catalog of subjects covered in those tapes. A quick scan of such a catalog could at least reveal the range and depth of those sessions, enough maybe to allow a fast synthesis and give me a mental snapshot of the trouble with Karen.

I found no such catalog, nor could I locate a case file, which should at least show a psychiatric profile of the patient as well as progressive commentaries by the doctor.

I did find a little leatherbound notebook in the bookcase headboard of Powell's bed. It was not labeled and the contents were written in what appeared to be some sort of shorthand notation. Scrutiny revealed the shorthand to be, actually, an abbreviated form of plain English; further scrutiny satisfied me that the forty-odd pages of jottings all concerned Karen Highland. I added this to my treasure trove.

Ten more minutes of careful searching turned up several more notebooks, a couple of unmarked cassette tapes, a small desktop appointment calendar covered with doodles and more shorthand, a couple of bankbooks that indicated that the five-year residency had been profitable, indeed, for Doctor Powell, two one-way airline tickets to Rome for the following Saturday, a small legal tract on "Conservancy and the Mentally Disabled," and ten thousand dollars worth of American Express traveler's checks in Powell's name.

I took the notebooks, tapes, and calendar and left everything else undisturbed.

And now I have to give you one of those "suspended disbelief" items. I do not know how to explain it in conventional logic nor even in a sensible unconventional logic; I can only tell you what occurred, or how I sensorially interpreted what occurred, and leave it to your own conclusions.

As I was standing at the front door and preparing to quit that apartment, I saw something suspended in the air over near the bookshelves in the sitting room. Now, the room was darkened, with only a small nightlight near the front door, so this object or whatever had to be supplying its own illumination. It had a very faint glow, somewhat like radium, and exhibited a sort of undulating-wave appearance—if you can visualize a sheer curtain panel being gently manipulated by the breeze at an open window, sort of

119

like that except that no constant form was maintained.

The closest description I can arrive at, for those who may have had a class or two in psychics, is that it looked like an electronic screen representation of the electrical field of an energy wave, with about the same degree of stability—at maximum expansion, maybe ten inches wide and two feet long.

As I watched, this energy wave or whatever moved into the bookcase and instantly contracted to a point and disappeared. As it did so, a large volume was ejected from the bookcase and fell to the floor.

I stood rooted to my spot by the door for perhaps thirty seconds, then I turned the lights back on, went to the bookcase, picked up the fallen book.

It was warm to the touch, front and back, a heavy leatherbound tome titled "Principles of Economics."

What appeared at first to be a bookmark tucked between the pages turned out to be two sheets of lined yellow notepaper, legal size, folded twice and filled front and back with finely scrawled handwriting.

The heading of the front sheet read: "The True Final Will and Testament of Joseph Quincy Highland."

The second sheet was headed: "My Dearly Beloved Karen."

Let me tell you that, even before I read those final messages from JQ, my mind was fairly tumbling with the implications of the event.

Please remember that I am a guy who does not like any suggestion that supernatural agencies could be at work in my reality. Yet I had been given an at-hand demonstration of an event that seemingly could not be explained in any other terms.

From somewhere out of the matrix that separates the world of space and time from whatever other realities may be only dimly guessed, an entity of will had found a way to interact with the energy universe and to thereby place in my hands the desires and instructions of a man more than ten years in his grave.

Ashes to ashes . . . okay.

But evidently something far more meaningful than ashes just goes right on truckin'.

CHAPTER SIXTEEN
Roots

I used a small copier in Powell's study to copy JQ's final papers, then returned the originals to the book and replaced it in the bookcase, with the thought that since it had remained undetected there all those years, that would be the safest storage for the time being.

Having only Marcia Kalinsky's words as a guide, I had no way of knowing just how significant this "true final will" might actually be—and, actually, it was only a rather informal codicil to what obviously must have been an involved and intricate formal will, considering the dimensions of that estate.

Marcia had told me, you may recall, that JQ had spent the last two years of his life reorganizing his estate in such a way that "most everything would go directly to Karen instead of to his own son." Since there had also been talk of a "trust" from Karen, I had assumed that the bulk of the estate had gone into that trust, which is a more or less standard operating procedure for bequests to minor children. The "trust," in that sense, is designed to preserve the estate and to expand it as much as possible through wise investments until such time as the heir is deemed mature enough to take responsibility for his own business affairs, meanwhile providing income adequate to maintain a certain desired standard of living. A trustee is appointed to manage that trust at the time that the trust is created on paper—in this case, according to Karen, our friend Terry Kalinsky—and it was my understanding that such an appointment is not dependent upon confirmation by a probate court, as it is for an executor. When the trustor dies, then, the trustee takes over as irrevocable agent for the trustor in carrying out the terms of the trust and as sort of a financial guardian for the beneficiary.

The setting up of a trust is of course a very intricate legal procedure, with all sorts of ramifications having to do with inheritance taxes, probate expenses, that sort of thing. For holdings as massive and as extensive as Highland's, the intricacies must have approached infinite mass. But I could only imagine all that, having no actual knowledge of any of it.

Being only "almost a lawyer," moreover, I could not fully evaluate the possible effect of a hand-scrawled death-bed codicil upon such a mass of highly formulated estate planning; indeed, I would go so far as to suggest that few highly competent lawyers would hazard a guess on that score even with all the papers in front of them. The final determination would have to be made by a probate court and the legal skirmishing in that arena could consume years of court calendars.

So I really did not know what I had, there. The flow of events following JQ's death, such as they were, would seem to have reduced or perhaps totally neutralized any significance to Karen, herself, but if a legal basis could have been established in time, the codicil could have had tremendous significance to Kalinsky—and perhaps it still could.

Marcia had told me, remember, that JQ had spent the final two years of his life reorganizing the estate. If that were true, and the codicil seemed to more or less verify that by implication, then obviously the dying old man had a last-minute change of heart.

I am going to reproduce for you, here, the full text of that death-bed wish, "The True Last Will and Testament of Joseph Quincy Highland:

> Let it be known by these presents that although I am of rapidly deteriorating body, I am of sound and rational mind and not under the influence of alcohol, narcotics or medications of any kind whatsoever; being of sound mind and in excellent possession of all mental faculties, I do set my will and desires to this writing in full knowledge of my imminent departure from this lifetime, perhaps within the next several hours; I do hereby with full faculties intend that this writing be regarded as a legally binding and governing document that shall serve to modify any and all provi-

sions of any and all extant documents executed by me during my lifetime having to do with the distribution of my worldly assets upon my death, but does not and shall not serve to invalidate wholly or to replace wholly such documents but only those provisions that are in conflict with or inconsistent with the desires herein expressed, to wit:

It is my death-bed wish that all my worldly assets except the First Trust established for the benefit of my Granddaughter, Karen Elena Highland, shall upon my death pass directly to my son, Thomas James Highland, and I do hereby nominate my son, Thomas James Highland, as sole executor of my estate.

I do also hereby and specifically remove as Trustee for my Granddaughter's First Trust Terrance Kellan Kalinsky and do hereby appoint in his place my son, Thomas James Highland, as sole Trustee of the First Trust established for the benefit of my Granddaughter, Karen Elena Highland.

Lest there be any doubt as to my wishes so stated above, I do hereby expressly and specifically declare all other Trusts, save the First Trust named above, to be canceled and voided as though they had never been drawn; all other bequests, save those named above, are likewise canceled and voided as though they had never been made.

The codicil was signed and dated on the day that I later determined was JQ's last day on earth.

There also were two witnessing signatures, those of Bruno and Tony Valensa. Figure that one.

Considering the fact that TJ had passed on shortly after JQ, and since Karen was TJ's only natural heir, probably, it would seem on the surface that this newly discovered document—even if admitted to probate—would have no real impact on the final settlement of the estate. Unless, of course, there could be claims against TJ's estate, which could be considerable if the bulk of JQ's estate had passed to the son before TJ's death—and that would knock the whole thing into a cocked hat—especially if Elena had family somewhere and taking into account California's community property law.

The most striking feature, of course, was the impact on Kalinsky. This guy had, for the past eleven years or so, occupied the catbird seat from which old JQ, in his final hours, had sought to eject him.

Forget for the moment about bequests, large or small, and just consider that the executor of an estate can reasonably expect to collect two to three percent of the total assets for his services. The executor of an estate with the value and complexity of this one may even be deemed by the probate court to be worthy of a larger slice, but take just three percent of the Highland assets and we are talking a chunk of money.

The term *billion* has no real correspondence in the mind, the value so indicated being such a high number as to place outside normal human usage. In the

United States, it means a thousand millions. Think of that. Three percent of just one billion produces a figure of thirty million, and we are talking U.S. dollars. We are also talking the root of all evil, as some would have us believe, and I was looking at roots entangled and running everywhere.

Even the Internal Revenue Service was having trouble trying to determine just how many billions old Joe was worth.

It was all too murky for my quick assimilation, and I was staggering about in the dark, anyway, since I really had no idea whatever as to the actual legal status of the estate. I had been given casual generalities and a very limited understanding of the relative positions of all the players in this drama.

Karen, herself, had been vague and apparently disinterested in everything except her immediate problem, or what she perceived as her problem.

Kalinsky had actually told me nothing whatever but had simply conducted himself in a manner that would lead to the natural presumption that he was in charge and running things.

The interview with Marcia had produced more tangible information than I had gained anywhere else, and even that was suspect.

My tap on the federal computers had given me the understanding that the estate was still in probate, yet everyone at Highlandville seemed to be preparing for the big turnover on Karen's twenty-fifth birthday, one short week away. So maybe the federal data banks were running a bit behind; if that were true, it would then be an indication that the estate had been settled in very recent times. I cannot believe that the IRS would stand by and allow that transfer unless they already knew the dimensions of their own share; likewise the State of California and various other agencies with fingers in the pie.

So I had to martial the facts and attempt to draw my own picture since circumstances simply did not allow me the luxury of a liberal education in the matter.

Before I do that here, though, I want to give you JQ's last words to his "Dearly Beloved Karen:"

> You are too young and I too old and limited in time to fully explain the peculiar exigencies which have moved my hand this night toward your continued protection under my love. Just be aware and one day when you are older try to understand that my motivation in this action is solely toward your ultimate benefit and to shield you from a very real danger that I, in my physically diminished state, am otherwise powerless to oppose.
>
> I wish also to request of you a particular favor, as a testament of our love for each other, that you remove from my soul a most grievous burden that I simply cannot carry to my grave: love your mother, Elena, as I have loved you, and do your best to give back to her that which I took from her without just cause, understanding in your heart of hearts that all her supposed sins are instead my sins and all

her failures my failures and all her weak-
nesses my weakness.

Give back to her, Dear Karen, all that which
you alone now have the power to give.

Good-bye, My Darling. We shall meet again,
one beautiful day, beyond the stars.

Powerful stuff, eh. It was even more powerful in
the original script. And I was beginning to love this
old man, this reclusive, eccentric billionaire who'd
had the power to install kingdoms and reshape the
economics of earth—to feel a particular kind of pity
for him, also.

With all that power, and all that apparent wisdom,
and all that love, he had nevertheless managed to
totally screw up his own family.

And, yeah, I knew why that book had been ejected
from its resting place of eleven years. But why me,
Joe? Shit. Why me?

CHAPTER SEVENTEEN
A Fix for Karen

My pool buddy, the bartender, was lurking about outside my door when I returned to my room. He was agitated, very apprehensive, and lost no time on pleasantries.

"Need to talk to you, Mr. Ford," he almost whispered.

I opened the door and ushered him inside, wondering what the hell.

Turns out his name is Paul Ramirez. He has worked at the Highland estate for the past couple of years, more or less. Guy of about twenty-eight, good looking, a Latino male in his prime and showing it, well set up, intelligent, still lives at home with his parents though occasionally "stays over" at Highlandville when an occasion demands. He was supposed to be staying over this weekend, but had decided that he could not do that.

"There's a bunch of cops downstairs," he explained. "They're interviewing all the help and I can't handle that right now. Don't get me wrong, I don't have any kind of criminal problem, I mean nothing serious. But there are some bench warrants out on me, traffic tickets I never took care of, and they're gonna put my ass in jail if they catch it before I have the money to settle the tickets."

I knew there was something more than traffic tickets behind his encampment at my door, but I played along. "How much do you need?" I asked him.

"Oh no, please, don't think I came here to hit you up. That's going to take three or four hundred bucks, with all the penalties and interest. 'Course, I could use a few bucks to hit the beach for a while, let this thing cool. I noticed awhile ago all the questions you were asking, then when the cops came—and I've heard the talk around here tonight so I get the idea you're trying to help Miss Highland. Listen, she's an okay lady, she gets my vote, I don't think she could have done something like that. Point is, I have some information that could be very important to her and I thought, since I can't go to the cops, not right now . . ."

"You need a few bucks to hit the beach for a while."

He showed me a nervous smile. "Yes sir."

I had a couple of fifties and small change in my wallet. I gave him the fifties, then wrote him a check for five hundred dollars, pushed it at him, said, "Go down first thing Monday and clear up that traffic problem. Write down my telephone number before you cash the check. Start calling me Monday afternoon every hour on the hour until you get me. Miss

Highland is going to need all the help she can get. Think of the five hundred as a very small down payment on her gratitude if you can help her out of this mess. Understand me?"

He replied, "You bet, sir, I sure understand you."

I said, "Okay, right now we are probably on very limited time. What do you have for me?"

He came right back with: "Bad blood between Doctor Powell and Mr. Kalinsky."

I said, "Do tell."

"Yes sir. They had a hell of a beef just about a week ago—in fact, yeah, just last Saturday. I was inside stocking the bar and I heard them in the hallway just outside the lounge. I ducked down behind the bar just because I was embarrassed, not because I was trying to spy on anybody. I just . . ."

I said, "Sure. Anyway . . ."

"Anyway, nothing was said about Mrs. Kalinsky, but I think that's what the beef was about. I mean, it's no great secret around here that Doctor Powell and Mrs. Kalinsky had this thing going."

"This thing . . . ?"

"Yes sir, you know, they've been playing around together."

I said, "Everybody knew that, huh?"

"All the service force, I guess, yes sir. What you don't see as a bartender or waiter, Mr. Ford, I mean—we're right there buried in all that stuff, but everybody thinks we're blind and deaf or something, except to wait on them. Hell, we see it all. We hear it all."

"Exactly what did you hear during this beef between Powell and Kalinsky?"

"Well, let's see, the doctor is the one that is so burned. Mr. Kalinsky was just very cold and hard. I only heard about half of what he said. The doc I could hear loud and clear, he was really shouting. He said something like, 'You can threaten me all you like but you can't pull my strings any longer.' Strings, like a puppet, see. He says, ' . . . outrageous . . . ' but I don't know what was outrageous, and then, 'I'll be out of here in two weeks and that's final! Do your damnedest!' "

I asked, "And what did Kalinsky say to that?"

"He says, 'You'll go out alone and naked, then. And maybe feet first.' "

"He said that?—maybe feet first?"

"Yes, sir, and the doctor got that meaning. He said that he had enough on Mr. Kalinsky to send him up for life, that he had all the evidence hidden away somewhere and that it would all come out if he died, that Mr. Kalinsky had better take great pains to see that he never died—I mean that Doctor Powell never died."

"What did Kalinsky say to that?"

"He laughed, Mr. Ford. He laughed. Then he said, 'Take her to hell with you, then.' I think he meant Mrs. Kalinsky. But did you see the way he carried on with her down by the pool tonight? When he thought she was dead?"

I said, "Yeah, I noticed that. You didn't hear Miss Highland's name mentioned during that argument?"

"No sir. I think they were talking about Mrs. Kalinsky."

"Is that all you recall about the argument?"

"That's about it, yes sir. But if something else should come to me ..."

I walked Ramirez to the door and told him, "Get cool somewhere. Don't mention any of this to anyone else until you've checked back with me. But get straight with the cops on that traffic thing. We may need to lay this on them."

"I understand, Mr. Ford."

At the door, I inquired, "Why did you come to me instead of going to Kalinsky with this?"

He chuckled nervously. "Kidding? That guy is cold as ice. My car would have lost its brakes or something on the way home."

I said, "You really feel that way?"

He shivered as he replied, "Bet your ass I do. I knew you were an okay guy, though. You learn to spot them quick, in my business. Especially the assholes. They turn up quick."

I smiled and said, "I guess that means that mine did not turn up."

"You are absolutely right, Mr. Ford, it did not," he assured me.

I hit him with what I thought would be one last question before turning him loose into the night. "How do you really feel about Miss Highland?— straight shit, now."

"Straight shit, sir," he replied, "she's almost too good to be true—I mean, for a rich person. To tell the truth, I've been in love with her for two years. Sort of a hopeless fantasy—you know? But I'll bet I could get rid of those spells for her."

"How would you go about doing that, Paul?"

"I'd love her in the morning and I'd love her in the night, maybe all night long."

"You think that would fix her, huh?"

"Yes sir, I think it would."

If only, I was thinking, that could be true.

CHAPTER EIGHTEEN
Upgrading

It was a little past two o'clock. Karen had been returned home and put to bed. A security man called Gallo was in occupation of her sitting room. He assured me that he was a "quite competent" paramedic and that she was "okay" but was not to be disturbed. I accepted that, for the moment, and went in search of Kalinsky.

I found him in the lounge, having coffee with two very relaxed and friendly plainclothes cops. I had not noticed either of these at the death scene. I shook hands with them under Kalinsky's introductions and joined the table for coffee.

I was introduced by name only, but the cops apparently already had me related. One of them said something sympathetic with regard to the "hell of a night."

The four of us small-talked for another minute or so, Kalinsky all sad charm and quiet grace, then the cops made pleasant farewells and departed.

That left just Kalinsky and me in the lounge,

except for a houseman hovering inconspicuously in the background. Kalinsky's demeanor underwent a marked alteration the instant the cops walked away, moving in a twinkle from charm and grace to nasty hard.

"Let's get an understanding right up front here," he growled at me. "You don't do diddly-squat around here unless you check it out with me first, especially anything involving outside authorities."

It was a time for hardball and I was entirely ready for that game. "Get screwed," I growled back. "I have not signed your dumb-ass contract and I do not intend to. So let's upgrade this understanding. You back off and come at me like a regular guy and maybe I will hang around long enough to straighten out this mess you've got here."

"Oh pardon me," he said, the sarcasm dripping, "I forgot myself. You're the miracle man, aren't you—creeping Jesus himself, and you're going to forgive all our sins."

I replied, "The hell I am," and got to my feet. "I'll just catch up with the cops for a safe escort out of this nuthouse."

He grabbed my arm and held on. Our eyes locked briefly while I was deciding whether or not to break his arm off at the elbow and take it with me, then he flashed me a twinkle and said, chuckling, "You're right, I'm being an ass. Sit down, let's talk like adults."

He removed his hand. I sat down. We each lit a cigarette. He blew smoke straight up and said, in a musing tone, "You've met me at my worst, Ash.

Sorry. Everything has just been too crazy. I was upset because you called the cops before you called me. If you had routed it through me, see—well, we have channels, friends. We would have had the right people on the response and we could have avoided that circus out there."

I replied, in about the same tone, "I understand. But you need to understand my problem too. You are not my client. Karen is. And I am not that sure that your friends are also Karen's friends. So you should understand my desire to have a neutral response."

"I understand that now," he said softly. "I did not understand it a moment ago. Again, I apologize. I thought you had simply lost your head and called the cops without thinking through the consequences. I was hoping to impress upon you the importance of working through channels."

I said, "Well, now that we have that all straightened out . . ."

"Yes," he replied in a soft voice, "but it is not completely straightened out. You see, you are working a false hypothesis. Karen is not your client. In fact, Ash, you have no client here, as such. You serve entirely at my pleasure. Karen does not have the power to engage you or anyone else in her direct service. You work for me or you do not work here."

I knew about where he was coming from, but I wanted him to say it, flat out. I told him, "Karen has all the power she chooses to exercise. She can run your ass out of here any time she wishes to do so. I have been considering advising her to do just that."

He was still smiling, but a hard edge was developing at the eyes. "Why are you acting this way? You must know that Karen would be in a cell right now if I had not intervened."

I shrugged and said, "One cell is much like another. And it occurs to me, Kalinsky, that this whole thing has come to a head at a highly convenient time for you. The Highland estate obviously cannot pass into the control of a mental incompetent, can it? In fact, your cup of convenience seems to be fairly running over. In one fell swoop, here tonight, you've perpetuated your grip on the Highland billions while also ridding yourself forever of a troublesome teammate who also happened to be a competitor for your wife's affections. So surely you can understand why I am acting this way. Would Karen be in a cell right now but for your intervention? I wonder. I have to wonder, Kalinsky, if it was your intervention that put her in the shadow of that cell in the first place."

I don't know what sort of reaction I had expected from the guy. I only know that I was a bit surprised at the one I got. He seemed to relax, sink a bit lower in his chair, smiling inwardly. After a brief silence he laughed softly and gave me a wink.

"Well," he said quietly, "we seem to be getting all the cards onto the table. Incidentally, I just remember that I did not express my gratitude to you for saving Marcia's life. That was a hell of an heroic thing. I salute you. But don't think for a minute it gives you room to tweak my nose. I won't stand still for that. Are you really psychic?"

It seemed that we were moving back into a game

of verbal tennis. I told him, "I have my moments. As for Marcia, it was not heroic, just human, and you expressed your gratitude in the only way that counts by your actions at poolside. You're really in love with the lady, aren't you?"

He looked at his hands as he replied. " 'Course I'm in love with her. She's the only thing that made these past twenty years bearable. Think it's been a picnic here, submerging my entire life in someone else's business? You said a cell is a cell. Look at mine, Ash. My whole life is a cell. Just how good a psychic are you?"

I said, "I found Karen. How good was that?"

"Damned good," he came right back. "I meant to ask you how you did that."

"It did me," I told him. "And quick enough to spoil the timing on the play. No way would Karen or Doc Powell either one get that far away on foot in the time allowed. How long have you had that conservancy tucked away for such convenient use?"

"Who said they got there on foot?"

"I didn't notice wings on either of them."

Kalinsky gave me a sly grin. "Wings would be nice. But a car is faster. The police found Carl's BMW in the bushes just a few hundred feet beyond that canyon. As for Karen, she had plenty of time to wander that far. I spent more than ten minutes searching for her on premises before I alerted you and Carl. Maybe that canyon is one of Karen's favorite getaways and maybe Carl knew that. Maybe you knew it, too, which also disposes of the psychic bullshit. Who says I've had anything tucked away?"

I said, "Your telephone conversation with a certain judge says it, the one you made before you came out to the scene."

His eyes narrowed. He crushed out his cigarette and immediately lit another, toyed with his coffee cup, finally said to me, "You're a pretty good fisherman but a lousy psychic."

I said, "Other way around, TK. But never mind, neither applies here. I'm also a pretty good detective. Matter of fact, though, it does not take much of a detective to catch the action around here. Why was Carl leaving?"

Kalinsky was a bit slow moving to the opposite corner to return that serve. He bit his lip for a nervous moment before replying. "Did he tell you that?"

It was a weak return, and it caught me off balance. I could have offered a better volley than this: "No. We were talking about God and Satan when you came in on us. Trying to decide who's in charge here."

"I'm in charge here," said my host immediately. "Don't forget it. And don't take too many liberties with my patience. You may be a high-mucky guru in certain circles, but you're small change in this division, kid."

So the hell with it. I went back to hardball. I said, "I was supposed to be Karen's victim, wasn't I? You ran me through your gristmill and decided I'd make the perfect turkey. That's the only reason you allowed Karen the freedom to cultivate me. Carl sent her to Zodiac for the specific purpose of finding a cuckoo to crucify. Then he got cold feet or an attack of conscience and wanted out. Adding insult to injury, he was going to take Marcia with him. That little subplot came to a head down beside the pool tonight, when you thought you'd lost Marcia the hardest way and you realized how much she really meant to you. Ipso quicko, that emotional head of steam sent Carl to the crucifix in my place. A brilliant move, sure, in the short look—but you should never let a momentary emotion replace years of careful planning, TK. It's all coming unglued, now, the timing shot to hell—and then, also, there is this small change rattling around in the basement and threatening to bring the billions tumbling down."

Kalinsky growled, "You're crazy as hell."

I told him, "Not as crazy as you think, if you believe I walked into this mess unprepared." It was time to make a believer of him. "Karen has not killed anyone. She has not tried to kill anyone. She is not mentally incompetent. She shall not be deprived of her rightful inheritance."

I produced the Xeroxes of JQ's final papers from beneath my shirt and slid them across the table to him. And I lied a little. I do that, sometimes, in a good enough cause.

"The originals of these papers are in legal hands and will be formally recorded with the probate court on Monday morning. There will also be an emergency motion to have you removed from further influence over Karen, plus a change of venue to an impartial judge. Then we'll all discover who is really in charge here, kiddo."

Kalinsky was giving me a stunned, sick look—even before he picked up the papers. He muttered, "We've been eleven years closing this thing. It's scheduled for formal conclusion in less than a week. You can't..."

By this time he knew what he was holding in his hands. They were shaking somewhat as he scanned down the lines of spidery handwriting. He did a quick scan of both papers, then went back for a close reading, and he did that twice before he pushed his chair back, refolded the papers, and slid them back to me.

He said, very quietly, "If this is fraudulent..."

I said, just as quietly, "You know it's not. If anybody could recognize JQ's handwriting, it should be you."

He sighed and admitted, "It looks like his. 'Course, it would take an expert opinion."

I said, "I'm sure it will pass muster."

He sighed again. "Yeah... probably. Well, shit. This makes me feel like hell, you know. All these years... Thought I enjoyed JQ's confidence. Looks like... Well, hell, makes no difference to Karen, all comes out the same, anyway. Except—well, shit, Ash—this will just muddy everything up again if you introduce this thing at this point."

I replied, "Probably."

"And it would place Karen in great peril if you try to challenge the conservancy."

I said, "Maybe."

"Well, maybe we could come to some..."

I said, "Maybe we could."

"I don't give a shit about the money."

I said, " 'Course not."

"Really, I'm sincere about that. Won't make that much difference, anyway, not to me. Time for the turnover, anyway. I've earned my fees. I don't see how a court in the land would take them away from me at this point. But, for Karen's sake . . ."

I said, "For her sake, right."

"What would it take to persuade you to keep this out of public view until the probate formally closes? That's only a few days from now."

I told him, "I would have to be persuaded that I am really a lousy detective and that my scenario is all wrong, that our interests are identical."

"They are," he assured me, "if you're talking about being on Karen's side."

I said, "That's what I'm talking about."

The guy really looked like hell. He was coming apart, for whatever reason. I felt a movement of sympathy for him—a movement tempered, however, by the unknown factors.

His eyes were watering. He produced a handkerchief and delicately blew his nose into it, carefully refolded it, and returned it to a pocket.

"How can I persuade you?" he asked humbly.

I said, "Believe that my only interest is to arrive at the truth of Karen's situation. Help me find that truth. If I then decide that she is in proper hands, here, and that the proper things are being done for her, then I will fold my tent and leave you all in peace."

Kalinsky dabbed at his eyes with a knuckle and said, "Fair enough. Where do we start?"

"We start with the truth," I told him.

"That," he said with a sigh, "is going to be damned difficult to find. And it just might knock both our socks off, if we ever get there."

I would remember, later, that he told me that.

CHAPTER Nineteen
Dimensions

So that you may know where I was coming from, and with what: I had felt that it was vital that I secure some degree of cooperation from Kalinsky, even if I had to club him to get it, and even if his reaction was only an appearance of cooperation.

Consider the circumstances at this point in the case. My client had been formally accused of manslaughter and, although she had been released and returned home pending some adjudication of the crime, the very nature and terms of her release actually placed her farther beyond my reach than if she had been jailed. Certain constitutional protections accompany any suspect into a jail cell; she could have legal counsel, proclaim her innocence, begin some sort of defense. In this particular situation, with Kalinsky the jailer, Karen had no rights whatever but was totally dependent upon the good intentions of her jailer as to her ultimate fate.

It is important that you understand the fine legal shadings of the situation. There was not going to be a "trial"—there would never be a trial in which Karen's guilt or innocence would be determined or even examined. The adjudication would be no more than a closed-door hearing, presided over by a judge—not a jury—the central focus of which would be to rubber-stamp an already existing legal determination that Karen Highland is not mentally competent to answer charges on any criminal complaint. In its very essences, this would be almost purely an administrative procedure and Karen would be remanded to the care and "protection" of her legal conservator.

Now this could be good—very good—or it could be very, very bad—depending upon the dimension of reality in which it is cast. I am not knocking the law—it is a good one, when not abused. If Karen wad, indeed, mentally incompetent, then she deserved that sort of protection—and especially so if she was indeed guilty of felonious behavior.

On the other hand, thought, if she was not incompetent and had committed no crime, then the net effect of all this would be to place her under the total domination of the person most likely to be the actual criminal.

I had to dimension Kalinsky as a rat if only because the theory was so pure and the coup so perfect—but there were other reasons, as well. Suffice it, for now, to say that I had my guard up all the way during the interchange that follows, that I was merely probing for truth and hoping to recognize it when it hit me—that I was simply trying to dimension the reality.

Bear in mind, too, that Kalinsky is a very sharp cookie. He was probably playing me at the same time that I was playing him; buying time, the same as me; looking for advantage, the same as me.

Assuming for the moment that he is, indeed, a rat, then both considerations+time and advantage—were vital to us both, whether or not he had actually bought my bluff regarding the death-bed will. In the rat dimension, he has had the luxury of eleven years of time to painstakingly manipulate events, and he is now within hours of his goal. These hours now, however, could be the undoing of the previous eleven years; one fumble, one wrong step, and it could all come tumbling down to engulf him.

It is not that I am so impressive an opponent, it is simply that I am there and he has not yet been able to "handle" me, therefore I am an unknown factor—a slippery surface, so to speak, upon which he has decided to test each step before consigning his weight to it. So he is playing me carefully, thinking maybe that he just needs to waltz me through another thirty-six hours or so and then he is home clean.

Or, in the other dimension, the same reasoning applies. In this reality, Kalinsky is a devoted and dedicated servant, convinced or at least fearful that his hard work of many years is coming to the final test under the most disheartening of circumstances, and he is trying valiantly to hold it together to the finish line. Again, I am there, too, an unknown factor that could be fortune-hunting for itself—and he needs only to stall me through and fake me out while he end-runs the scoring drive.

All this I am aware of. I am also aware that I must manipulate him while he thinks that he is manipulating me, otherwise I am outside the walls and out of play.

In the time dimension, I am more at tension than he. He is holding a pat hand while I bluff with jacks up and nothing whatever in the hold; he can call this bluff at any time while I must wait for fresh cards to tell my tale. Time is on his side, each tick of the clock taking him closer to victory; it is aligned against me, each tick carrying me farther into the wilderness of Karen's despair.

I beg your indulgence in all this exposition. I want the ting to develop for you as it developed for me, so I felt it necessary to put you in step with my own feelings, the understanding that accompanied me into this surprising discussion with Terry Kalinsky.

Is he a rat or is he a saint? Which dimension are we exploring here? I give it to you as it came to me, for your personal determination.

It is now close to three o'clock on that Sunday morning at the Highland estate. By mutual agreement, and for obvious reasons of privacy, we have moved to Kalinsky's office. The houseman has brought coffee and pastries because both of us missed dinner and the temple must be served.

Kalinsky is now coming at me like a regular guy— on the surface, anyway—and I am responding likewise. He has been perusing, once again, JQ's final thoughts while munching Danish. The conversation begins, in its substance, at this point.

—**Kalinsky**: "Can't get over this. Just can't get

over it. Okay, if he didn't want me, okay, but hell, I'd have to think he was of unsound mind to tap TJ for the job."

—**Me:** "His own son, though."

—**Kalinsky:** "I don't mean inheriting, I mean executor and trustee. Hell, I always did think it was wrong to cut TJ out. I mean, he was provided for, sure, but not in any way he could call his soul his own. So I'm not bitching about this. It sets things right. As for inheriting, I mean. But TJ never took any interest in business. Doubt he could even read the Dow and tell you what it meant. How'd you get this, by the way? Bruno give it to you?"

—**Me:** "Why Bruno?"

—**Kalinsky:** "Well, I noticed he witnessed. And Tony. Where the hell has it been all these years?"

—**Me:** "That's an interesting pair."

—**He:** "That's putting it mildly. Were those jerks sitting on this all these years? Why? I don't understand. Did he tell you?"

"Tell me what?"

"About the affidavit he and Tony filed?"

—**Me:** "I'd like to hear your version."

"No version to it. About four—no, maybe five years ago. They filed this affidavit saying they'd witnessed a late-hour change in the will. Claimed they didn't know what it contained because JQ had it covered up, exposed only the signature line. Said he died a few hours later and they never saw it again."

"No effect on the probate, though."

—**Kalinsky:** " 'Course not, how could it. There was a search, of course. We looked everywhere, talked to everyone who could have been in contact with him during those final hours, but . . . "

—**Me:** "Who all was that?"

—**He:** "The personal physician, now deceased. A nurse. One of the security boys and a couple of staff people. Oh, and Karen."

"And she was just a kid."

"Yeah. Not quite fourteen. Is she the one . . . ?"

—**Me:** "Anything significant you can see about the fact he had Bruno and Tony witness?"

—**Kalinsky:** "No, I guess that would be—they were with him all the time, his personal men, 'specially those last two years, night and day. Never saw such devotion. And not just because . . . "

—**Me:** "Huh?"

—**He:** "Very devoted. Guess you knew, they both had that problem."

"You mean, mute. Yeah. Family trait?"

—**Kalinsky:** "Something in the chromosomes, I guess. More than that, though, no disrespect meant, but more than that was wrong."

—**Me:** "The Valensas?"

—**He:** "Well . . . those two, anyway. A little slow, if you get me."

—**Me:** "What aren't you telling me?"

—**He:** "About what?"

—**Me:** "Valensa."

—**Kalinsky:** "Oh. Well . . . maybe you know already. Maybe not. Doesn't really make a shit not, I guess. They were Karen's uncles, only living relatives. Now there are none."

—**Me**, about twenty seconds later: "Elena's brothers."

—**He**: "Yeah."

—**Me**: "They had a take in that new will, TK."

—**He**: "Maybe so. Too bad they didn't produce it sooner, then. I told you, slow. Probably thought it would be disloyal to Karen."

—**Me**: "They didn't have the will."

—**Kalinsky**: "Who did, then?"

—**Me**: "JQ still had it."

—**He**: "Don't get you, there, Ash."

—**Me**: "You wouldn't, so let it slide. I'd like—"

—**Kalinsky**: "No, I want to know what you meant by that."

"You want to know who have me the will?"

"Yeah."

"JQ handed it to me."

Kalinsky, about thirty seconds later: "Aw... Don't play games. You mean...?"

—**Me**: "Literally, yeah. Only his hand was like an energy wave. It imbedded the hiding place and ejected the will. Fell at my feet. Pure energy. I could feel the heat from it."

—**He**: "I never believed in this shit. So don't think I'm calling you a liar. It's just..."

—**Me**: "Doesn't matter. Why did JQ oppose the Marriage?"

"What marriage?"

"Elana to his son. Was that before or after Bruno and Tony—?"

—**Kalinsky**: "No, after. Elena brought them here with her. She worked for JQ at first, personal secretary. That was before me. I came along a few years later. Way I got it, JQ didn't oppose the marriage. I believe he engineered it. Maybe a last desperate stab at making a man out of . . . "

—**Me:** "TJ?"

—**He:** "Yeah. Guy had problems, I guess. I used to hear stories, some of the staff snickering about him. I shut that off damn quick."

"What kind of stories?"

—**Kalinsky:** "Listen, if you're really on the level . . . I mean, do you—are you sincere about that? That energy wave thing?"

—**Me:** "Yep."

—**He:** "Well, the implications of that are just absolutely mind-boggling. Don't you think?"

—**Me:** "It used to boggle my mind. Still does, sometimes. What kind of stories?"

"You mean this kind of stuff is routine with you? Really?"

"More or less."

—**Kalinsky:** "So what you are saying—what this really means—if JQ could—shit, he's still living, somewhere. He's still aware, he knows what is . . . "

—**Me:** "Seems that way, doesn't it."

—**He:** "Do you believe that?"

—**Me:** "Is there some reason I should disbelieve it?"

—**He:** "Well, I mean . . . "

—**Me:** "The wisest men who have ever lived have almost with a single voice declared that the human soul is immortal. The problem, as I see it, is that a living soul needs to imbed itself into the energy universe before it can be made manifest in our reality. Since that normally occurs only during the phenomenon of sexual conception and parturition—the involvement with matter on this plane, I mean—we have come to think that any other method must be impossible. But how the hell do we know what is possible and what is not?"

—**Kalinsky**: "Well, Jesus . . . "

—**Me**: "Are you deliberately evading the stories about TJ?"

—**He**: "Well . . . it's embarrassing. I'd rather Karen never hear this."

—**Me**: "This is all in confidence, isn't it?"

—**Kalinsky**: "Oh, well, okay. Some of the staff claimed to have seen TJ strolling the grounds at night dressed like a woman."

—**Me**: "That, uh, by itself, doesn't mean a hell of a lot."

—**Kalinsky**: "JQ thought he might be queer."

—**Me**: "He actually voiced that to you?"

—**He**: "Not in so many words, no, but I could tell."

—**Me**: "Did you think that too?"

—**Kalinsky**: "I don't know what to think. TJ was not the kind of guy you ever got close to. Hardly knew him, yet I shared the same roof with him for about ten years. Yeah, ten years. Karen was three or four when I came on board. . . . they died . . . 'bout ten years later."

—**Me**: "How did they die?"

—**He**: "Is that a test question?"

—**Me**: "I'd be interested in your version."

—**Kalinsky:** "Carl told me that Karen thinks she killed them."

—**Me:** "How do you feel about that?"

—**He:** "All in her head, of course. Guilt, probably. She probably wanted Elena dead. When it happened that way, she translated it as—in her mind, she did it."

—**Me:** "She hasn't told me that."

—**He:** "She didn't tell me that, either. I'm telling you what Carl told me. Look . . . The official investigation said that gasoline vapors had collected inside the engine compartment and seeped into the main cabin, and that they ignited a few seconds after the engine was started. That's good enough for me. I accept that version."

—**Me:** "Have you shared that version with Karen?"

—**Kalinsky:** "Well, shit, it's general knowledge. I'm sure she has heard that version, sure she heard it at the time. I only just heard this thing from Carl a few weeks ago."

"Elena worked for JQ, you say? How long after she came here did she and TJ get together?"

"Less than a year, I think."

"Is all of this tied in with Carl's psychiatric profile of Karen? This family history thing?"

—**Kalinsky:** "Well, sure has to be. Elena was obviously highly unstable. Her brothers were, uh, well I hate to say it, but they were subintelligent."

—**Me:** "The thing, too, about TJ's little idiosyncrasies?"

—**He:** "I think it's mentioned in there."

—**Me:** "I would like to have a copy of that."

—**He:** "Sure. Get it for you tomorrow."

—**Me:** "I'd like to have it today."

—**Kalinsky:** "Sorry. The court has it. Only other copy is in the vault. Time-locked. Can't get to it until tomorrow."

—**Me:** "Why is JQ so disturbed about Elena?"

—**He:** "What?"

—**Me:** "The letter to Karen . . . he did Elena some terrible wrong. What was it?"

—**He:** "Christ, I don't know. Sounds that way, though, doesn't it?"

"How did Elena come this way in the first place?"

"I, uh . . . she was European . . . Castilian Spanish, I believe, yeah, spoke with an accent. But I . . ."

—**Me:** "She did have the power of speech, then."

—**He:** "Oh yeah, she wasn't affected by that. I forget what—seems like—I believe this defect shows up only in males but is transmitted by the mother. What do they call . . . ?"

"Did you get to know her? Before . . . ?"

"Not a lot, no. Very unstable. In and out of hospitals all that time. Threw some fits here, I remember, I mean real screamers. She got very violent."

—**Me:** "I'd like a look at her medical history too."

—**He:** "Shit, I wouldn't know where to look for it. JQ handled all that himself, personally, like he was ashamed of it, and I . . ."

—**Me:** "I guess he died ashamed of it. What if Elena was not, uh, unstable, TK?"

—**Kalinsky:** "Oh, shit, no, not that. He wouldn't do that. Not to Karen's mother."

—**Me:** "It would be a terribly heinous thing toe3"

—**He:** "Absolutely. He would not be capable of that. Look, JQ had his peculiarities and he was a hard businessman, but he was not an evil man."

—**Me:** "That would take an evil man."

—**He:** "Yes, it would, absolutely."

—**Me:** "Are you an evil man, TK?"

—**"Kalinsky:** "I swear to you, Ash, I am not. I am not an evil man. I could not do a thing like that."

—**Me:** "Not for all the money at Highlandville?"

—**He:** "How could I get that? I'm just a manager here. That's all I could ever be. The Highland money belongs to Karen. It will always belong to Karen, for as long as she's alive, anyway. Nobody can take it away from her. I sure as hell cannot take it away from her, and furthermore I do not want to. Look, I want out of it. I want out. And I am quite content to take my rightful share, my hard-earned share— which isn't shabby, believe me—and go be my own person. So if you think . . . "

Hell, I did not know what to think.

Or, I guess, maybe I just did not want to think what had to be thought about, at this point. But the dimensions of Karen's reality were beginning to fall more and more into a classic pattern. Obviously I would just have to climb in there with her and have a look around, for myself. And that, believe me, could be literally disastrous for both of us.

I told Kalinsky, "I want unrestricted access to Karen for the next twenty-four hours."

He said, "Okay, you got it."

I said, "I also want the psychiatric workup. And

don't tell me you can't defeat the time-lock. Get it. I absolutely have to have it, and right away."

He said, "Okay. You'll have it if I have to blow the damn doors. What else do you need?"

"An angel, maybe," I replied.

He grinned and told me, "Well it sounds like you've already found that."

And maybe I had. Yeah. Maybe so. Depending, of course, upon which dimension I was exploring.

CHAPTER TWENTY
Operating

It was quite an impressive package, that psychiatric workup, put together with a professional skill that had one foot in medicine and the other in law. Powell had done his homework quite thoroughly, and he even had two consenting opinions from outside shrinks "based on an exhaustive review of all pertinent data."

He had her principally diagnosed as a progressive paranoid schizophrenic with complications "ranging from dissociative tendencies toward multiple personality to latent nymphomania coupled to an Electra complex."

He cited family medical history, with great emphasis on Elena but only a passing ambiguity in reference to TJ and a single paragraph on Karen's uncles, whom he characterized as "constitutional inferiors."

And, yeah, the doc has been using hypnoanalysis with Karen. That could explain her vagueness about the relationship with her analyst, the suggestion that they were "just friends" and a denial that she had ever been "in analysis." Close bonding is a characteristic feature of the hypnoanalytic relationship; furthermore, it is a simple procedure to remove all conscious memory of such a session and, in fact, such a procedure is often used as a therapeutic feature.

The hypnosis angle could explain a lot of other troubling stuff too.

I sat at Powell's desk with the workup until I became aware of the dawn light edging the windows, then I shoved it aside with a sigh and just sat there with a blank mind and gazed out upon the lightening landscape for ten or fifteen minutes. I say "blank mind" because that is about what I was left with, at this point.

I frankly did not know what the hell to think. Emotion seemed to be working at me more strongly than intellectual reasoning—besides which the intellectual centers were becoming numb with fatigue and fuzzy with a growing anxiety.

So I sat there for ten or fifteen minutes and cooled the mind, turned up the right brain and dampened the left, gave the whole machine a little rest.

After that I felt a lot better—better enough to send to the kitchen for bacon and eggs and a pot of coffee—better yet, enough to tackle the shorthand in Powell's little notebooks while auditing the cassette tapes I'd found earlier.

The tapes turned out to be music and nothing else—Strauss, I believe—but the notebooks proved to be a code within a code, rambling phrases buried inside systematically abbreviated longhand, similar to the so-called Phillips Code used by Morse telegraphers in the old days to shorten wire time—duck soup, really, for the trained cryptoanalyst, which was one of my navy talents.

Duck soup, that is, with regard to the abbreviations, per se, but these were notes designed for communication only with the self who wrote them—sort of like memory-joggers—and I did not possess the memories to be jogged.

K wnts opr I took to mean "Kalinsky wants operator," but what the hell did that tell me?

Stl lngst bt cnt frvr hldby I would say is "Stall longest but cannot forever hold at bay"—so what?

It usually takes a leap of mind to overcome personal codes; you go for a logic system, and it helps to know a little something about the context of reality in which the notes are placed.

The trouble with leaping the mind is that sometimes you superimpose your own imagined reality upon the contextual reality of the noter to force an improper conclusion. But I was trying, and here is the way I leaped the two notes shown above:

"Kalinsky wants the operator. I will stall him as long as possible but I know that, sooner or later, I will have to give him the operator."

I will not burden you with the whole process. The above should give insight enough into the problems and uncertainties of such an endeavor—and to indicate that, after struggling for two hours with the Powell notes (this particular set from a notebook dated on the cover at just a few months prior to that moment) I still was left with more conjecture than certainty.

Even supposing that my construction of the "joggers" given above is accurate, I am still left with the question: what operator? Obviously he was not referring to a telephone operator.

We leap the mind, though, in a logic system that respects a contextual reality. So we put the above together with something that appears as *trbl brch pfsnl etcs* and *mk rbt KH* plus *bt wo pys bls?*"

This give us a "terrible breach of professional ethics—make a robot of Karen—but who pays the bills?"

Thusly a logical movement is formed, a mentality is frameworked, a conjecture takes shape as:

"Kalinsky has been after me to give him the operator. I will stall him as long as possible, but I know that, sooner or later, I will have to give it to him. And this places me in a hell of a dilemma. Not only is it a terrible breach of professional ethics, but it will make a robot of Karen. But, what the hell, after all, who is paying the bills around here?"

After that sort of synthesis, it takes no great leap to the "operator."

I already knew, or thought I knew, what Powell meant by that, but nowhere in the notebooks did this mysterious "operator" stand up and identify itself.

So I went to the scratch pads and calendars, the doodles, comparing Powell's with Kalinsky's—and that is how I found the operator. It appeared in both sets of doodles—repetitively in Powell's, only once but heavily outlined in truncated form in Kalinsky's.

I was shaking inside as I went down to the kitchen and personally supervised the putting together of a breakfast tray for Karen. It was now about eight o'clock. I was told that Kalinsky had gone to bed with orders that he not be disturbed until noon.

Marcia Kalinsky customarily slept until ten or eleven, often later on Sundays after a hard night at poolside; according to the poop in the kitchen, she had retired under sedation at about two o'clock and had left an order for poolside brunch at twelve-thirty.

I took the tray to Karen's apartment and told the sleepy-eyed watchdog to get lost.

He replied, "Sorry, sir, I was instructed to cooperate with you, but I am to remain at my post."

I said, "Move your chair to the hallway, then."

He was eyeing the breakfast tray with more than casual interest. I asked him, "Have you eaten yet?"

He said, "No sir, but I'm due to be relieved pretty soon."

I said, "Okay. Wait outside for him, though. And tell him to stay out there until I say otherwise. You can't expect Miss Highland to get up and move around with you guys lounging about in here."

He dropped his eyes and said, "Sure, I understand. She's still asleep, though." He glanced at his watch. "I gave her her last medication at four. She's due again."

I told him, "That's been changed. No more medication unless I say so."

"Mr. Kalinsky—"

"Wake him up, if you want to. But no more medication."

The guard/paramedic replied with eyes only and carried a chair into the hallway. I closed the door and locked it and took the tray into the bedroom.

The shades were drawn, the room in deep gloom. I opened it up to both light and air, went to the bathroom and dampened a small towel, sat on the bed and sponged her awake.

She was groggy from God knew what mixture of downer drugs and had a hell of time focusing on me, but I'm the stubborn type and I kept at her until it was obvious that she was functioning properly at the conscious level.

I forced strong black coffee on her and spoon-fed oatmeal and toast into her, then lit a cigarette and handed it to her. So far, not a word between us. The first ones came with the exhalation of smoke and in a very small voice. "I had a terrible dream."

"Tell me about it."

"I was ... walking ... it was night ... somewhere—oh, the trail, the trail to the little meadow. This ... monster—oh, a horrible monster—leaped out at me from the dark. Had fangs like ... like a werewolf or something, horrible yellow eyes, and it was ... frothing at the mouth. I hit it ... picked up something and hit it. When I ... did that ... it turned into Carl and ... and there was blood everywhere."

I took the cigarette from her and dragged on it, gave it back, said, "And then?"

"I ... don't know. It was all just ... very unpleasant. And endless."

"Endless, yeah," I said gloomily.

She sighed. "Yes." She looked about her, asked, "Who put me to bed?"

"You remember being put to bed?"

"Vaguely, yes. Or did I dream it? Did you . . . ?"

I grinned and shook my head. "Not yet. We have another problem to clear up, first. Do you remember what happened to Marcia last night?"

The great eyes clouded, fell. She took a thoughtful pull at the cigarette, gave me an oblique gaze and said, "Yes. She thought I did it. Did I do it?"

I asked, "Did you?"

She said, "How could . . . ? I wouldn't even know how to do that."

"Do you remember being there? At the pool? When she was drowning?"

"I . . . I'm not sure. There is some—I seem to have a picture of that but . . . I don't know if I'm remembering what she said or what I actually saw."

"Or something you dreamed?"

"I hope so. Is it a dream?"

I said, "Karen, our only touch with the world is through our minds. But all we ever really see is a shadow play, something that our mind interprets for us from sense excitations. Reality for you and for me, reality for every human being, is always a mental quality. The only way that we ever even know that a real world exists out there beyond the mind is when we compare our mental worlds with each other and find a correspondence. A dream is just another shadow play, except that it does not have its source in the outside world. That is why it is sometimes difficult to distinguish between something physically experienced and something only dreamed. Do you understand what I am saying?"

She replied, "I think so."

I continued, "Some dreams are so vivid, seem so real, that we actually store in memory phantom sense perceptions that are every bit as valid as an actual, physical experience. That is, we store odor memories, tactile memories, visual memories, auditory memories, just as though our dream had flesh—and, in remembering the dream, all those memories come flooding back with all the strength of a remembered actual event; sometimes stronger."

She said, "Yes, I . . ."

I was talking with two goals in mind. One, to stimulate her intellectually, make sure that she was mentally functioning; secondly, to provide a mental framework from which she might view her own confusions.

But I was leading her, really, into a confrontation with her "operator."

And I decided that the moment had arrived.

"For example," I continued, in the same conversational tone, "what if I were to ask you if you remember Elena Magdalena?"

Her eyes blinked rapidly, twice; a now-familiar expression spread quickly across her face, and she replied, in a normal voice, "Yes, I understand."

I watched her closely for a moment, then asked her, "What do you understand, Karen?"

She replied, without pause, "I will see as you say, hear as you say, think as you say, do as you say."

Son of a gun, as easy as that.

The girl was in a deep hypnotic trance, somnambulistic level. She was, indeed, a human robot. She would walk around with eyes wide open and all sensory apparatus fully functioning, yet with the objective functions of mind totally set aside, nothing but the receptive web of the subjective mind—or the subconscious—operative and awaiting instructions.

The "operator," here, was a simple auditory trigger keyed to a posthypnotic suggestion that, in effect, operated not only to return her instantly to deep trance but also, apparently, served as a transfer function—a transfer of control, that is, to whomever operated the trigger.

To test it, I told her in a purely conversational tone of voice, "You will awaken when I tell you to, and you will have no conscious memory that you have been in trance or that you have been given instructions. Nevertheless, after you have awakened and when you hear me say to you, 'Jump, Karen,' you will immediately go to the window and close it. If someone asks why you closed the window, you will explain that a storm is coming and that you do not want the rain to come in. Do you understand?"

She replied, sounding entirely natural, "Yes, I understand."

I said, "Wake up, then. Now."

With no visible alteration of her mood or demeanor, she said to me, "Yes, I have had dreams that seemed so vivid. I could actually smell the flowers and feel the fur on a squirrel."

She was right back where the earlier conversation had been interrupted. We chatted about dreams for a minute or two, and we both had some coffee and smoked cigarettes.

Then, very quietly, I said, "Jump, Karen."

She casually threw back the covers and got out of bed, slipped on a dressing gown, and went and closed all the windows that I had opened when I came in. She returned to the bed, removed the gown, lay down, and again picked up the conversation.

"Dreams are really neat, though. Sometimes better than . . ."

I said, "Why did you do that?"

"Why did I do what?"

"Why did you close the windows? Are you cold?"

She said, "No, but we don't want it raining in here, do we?"

I said, "Karen, it is not raining."

She replied, "It will be when the storm arrives."

I said, "What storm is that?"

She looked confused, and said, "Oh my. Did I dream that too?"

You see, there is a correlation there.

A corroboration, in fact, of the hypothesis I had been forming.

I quietly said, "Elena Magdalena," and put her back into that other reality.

Then, damn it, I had to figure the best way to get in there with her.

CHAPTER
TWENTY-ONE
Hypothesis

You need to have an understanding of the way hypnosis works if you are going to believe the rest of this story.

I doubt that anyone knows for sure precisely how or why it works, but those of us who have worked with it do not doubt that it does work, and sometimes in awesome ways.

So please bear with me a moment, while I refresh your understanding whether it needs it or not—and as only I, in my noncredentialed way, may approach the subject.

The human mind appears to be a duality of form, fit, and function (an old engineering term that works very well here) that manifests consciousness as the conscious and the subconscious minds, or the objective and subjective (psychology terminology), but which I prefer to consider a single force exhibiting various aspects at specific levels of activity (pure physics) to provide a totality of individual experience that we humans quantify as a living soul (metaphysical stuff).

This is not an auspicious beginning, is it?—but, remember, I asked you to bear.

One aspect of the duality has to do with reasoning power: How do we understand with the intellect what we perceive through the senses?

Psychologists and logicians alike recognize two basic modes of reasoning, the inductive and the deductive methods. Hypnosis theory tells us that the conscious mind is capable of both modes, but that the subconscious mind is capable only of deductive reasoning.

Let us examine that idea, since it is crucial.

Inductive reasoning is when you notice that little Johnny has bleary eyes, a runny nose, fever, and little red blotches about the skin, and you pick up the phone and tell Dr. Jones that Johnny has the measles.

You have taken various noted particulars and put them together into a general assumption: Johnny has the measles.

Dr. Jones receives this information, but is aware that you do not have a medical diploma and do not therefore belong to the AMA, so he asks you if Johnny has a fever, are his eyes bleary, and does he have little red blotches upon the body. He is exercising the deductive mode.

He has taken your general assumption and broken it back down into particulars.

In a well-organized human mind, both modes are operating pretty much all the time. If someone comes up to you and tells you that Johnny has the measles, and you look at Johnny, and he is exhibiting none of the symptoms of measles, you are probably going to disagree with that someone—at least until you take Johnny's temperature and look closely for spots.

Thus, between the two modes, you exhibit a certain ability to discriminate reality—what is true and what is false; you can exercise judgment.

In hypnosis theory, the subconscious is purely subjective and deductive. It cannot discriminate or judge sensation or even thought: in fact, it does not think, was not designed to do so except in a most elemental sense, is merely a plastic web, so to speak, on which is impressed instructions to the motor nerves and in which is stored the living memory.

In trance, so the theory goes, the conscious mind is shoved aside and the subconscious brought to the fore, under the direct influence of an outside mind, which imparts information directly onto the receptive, nondiscriminating subconscious web—which is always there and ready to serve, even in sleep—in effect bypassing the judgmental functions of the conscious, or thinking, mind.

So if you are in trance and I tell you it is very hot in here, you will sweat; if I say it is cold, you will turn blue and shiver; if I say you have the measles, and the trance is deep enough, you will break out in spots imitating the measles rash and you will probably run a fever and develop bleary eyes and all the other symptoms.

Your subconscious is thus responding dutifully to the stimuli placed in it and reasoning deductively to harmonize your body and your being with the truth it has been told, and it accepts every stimulus as "truth" without question or even the power to question, because this is what it is designed to do.

Form, fit, and function; conscious and subconscious designed to work as a team; aspecting all levels of human activity; a human soul growing into its own individual potential for what reason only God knows.

Curious thing about hypnosis, though. A subject in even the deepest trance does seem to exercise some sort of threshold judgment in matters very dear to the soul, suggesting that the duality of functions may not run as deep as may appear; the mind is still the mind, a cosmic entity, and it may be pushed just so far.

For example, a person who will not kill in the waking state cannot be forced to kill in trance. A truly chaste person awake is a chaste person in trance. The moral imperatives sometimes take a quirky twist, though: a hypnotized woman who disrobes entirely without a qualm under hypnotic demand balks at removing her wedding ring; a man with holes in his socks refuses to remove his shoes but picks up a dagger and attacks a dummy upon command; a minister of the gospel will tell ribald stories and agrees to sexual seduction but will not take the Lord's name in vain.

Most experimental hypnotists have discovered, though, that wiles succeed where strong-arms fail.

All sorts of bizarre effects may be produced by simple suggestion placed into the subconscious receptive. Through positive hallucination, an oak tree may appear beside the couch and the subject will describe the birds in it and even try to catch them if you ask him to.

Through negative hallucination, all the furniture in the office may disappear and the subject will wander around for hours seeking a place to sit down.

These effects may even be triggered or "operated" weeks or months following the registration of a posthypnotic suggestion, with the hypnotist nowhere about.

But I was speaking of wiles.

The woman who will not disrobe may be tricked into doing so through simple negative hallucination, by which she believes herself to be alone in the room and preparing for her bath.

The man who would abruptly awaken if ordered to kill may be tricked into picking up a knife and attacking the first person to enter the room if he had been told to expect a maniac who meant to murder his children and rape his wife.

Is your hypothesis already formed?

Are you ready to leap ahead of me, again, now? Please wait. You ain't seen nothin' yet.

CHAPTER
TWENTY-TWO
Communicating

"Can you hear me, Karen?"

"Yes, of course, I can hear you."

"Are you comfortable?"

"Yes, thank you, I am quite comfortable."

"Do you know who I am?"

"Yes."

"Who am I?"

"You are Ashton Ford."

"And who are you?"

"I am Karen Highland. . . ."

"Do I detect a certain confusion in that response?"

"Is that what you want?"

"I want the truth, Karen, always the truth. Do not let my questions become your answers. You are not to attempt to interpret what I want. You are always to reply truthfully, to the very best of your ability. Do you understand that?"

"Yes, I understand that."

"So, now, tell me . . . who are you?"

"I am Karen Highland. And . . . "

"Yes?"

"I don't know. I am Karen Highland."

"Okay, let's rest it awhile. Don't become agitated, just let it rest for now, but we are going to come back to it, so be ready. How old are you, Karen?"

"I will be twenty-five years old."

"Soon?"

"Yes, soon."

"Any anxiety about that?"

"No."

"Again, though, you seem a bit undecided about your age. I am going to ask the question again. I want you to think about it, very carefully, before you give me the answer. How old are you, Karen, in your totality of expression?"

"In my totality . . . "

"Yes."

"I will be twenty-five. I would be thrice that."

"Say that again."

"I will be twenty-five. I would be thrice that."

"Should we say, then, that there are two Karens?"

"If you want to say that."

"It is not what I want, dear. Give me the truth."

"How many Karens?"

"Yes."

"There is but one Karen."

"One Karen?"

"Yes."

"Let us put it this way, then. To the one Karen, how old are you?"

"I will be twenty-five."

"To the one who is not Karen, how old are you?"

"I would be thrice that."

I had stumbled into something hot, already, hardly a minute into the dialogue. There is an almost eerie quality to this particular type of session with a subject in very deep trance, at every time I have experienced it. The personality is there before you, spread open like a book, though the script is written in indecipherable symbols; you may turn the pages by verbal prompting, but only the personality under review may read what is written there.

So it is a game of wits in which you probe and the subject responds in usually a very direct and limited way. However, personalities even in deep trance will sometimes attempt to evade an honest response and may even openly resist or simply awaken if you get too close to a moral imperative. In that connection, please remember the discussion above.

This session with Karen is particularly eerie. She appears to be wide awake and our eyes often clash, but I am not dead certain as to who or what is behind those eyes.

"Let us tie this back to the earlier confusion, Karen, when I asked you to identify yourself, and let us place these responses regarding identity and age into a single package, then let us put that package away for the moment. When we come back to it, though, I will ask you only for the package and you will give me the package unscrambled in language that I will understand. Okay?"

"Okay."

"We will give that package a name. We will call

the package Highland. When I ask for Highland, you will open the package for me. Do you understand?"

"I understand."

"Who am I?"

"You are still Ashton Ford."

A bit of sarcasm there, see, even in deep trance. Eerie.

"Why did Karen seek out Ashton Ford and engage his services?"

"Why?"

"Yes. Why?"

"Because . . . Karen is in trouble."

Hell, I was not sure as to exactly whom I was dealing with now.

"Karen is in trouble?"

"Serious trouble, yes."

"How can Ashton Ford help Karen in this trouble?"

"He is doing so. Keep it up."

Eerie, yeah. I was not talking to Karen, now, though the voice seemed the same. Whomever I was working with, at this point, did not seem to be "in trance." Yet Karen definitely was in the deepest of trances.

"There is a sexual confusion?"

"Yes. But that is minor and easily overcome. You understand the problem, Ashton. Do not abandon her."

"To whom am I speaking?"

"You are speaking to Karen."

Yes, at that very moment, I was. This may seem very confusing—and I must admit to a certain confusion within myself, at this point, but already I was beginning to pick up the subtle nuances of the play unfolding here.

Let me see if I can explain it, as I was beginning to understand it, myself, in some coherent fashion. Karen was in hypnotic trance—probably as deep a trance as any I had ever witnessed. In that mode, her personality was spread before me in a most receptive state. I could ask it questions and it would respond, using Karen's regular motor functions as the vehicle of expression. But another personality, another entity that did not appear to have its source in that trance-receptive mind, was also present—perhaps no closer, physically, to Karen than I was, but nevertheless present and also using Karen's regular motor functions as a vehicle of expression.

If that sounds confusing to you, here, think of what it was doing to me, there.

"Are you still comfortable, Karen?"

"Yes."

"You have no discomfort or pain of any kind?"

"I have no discomfort or pain of any kind."

"That was not a suggestion. It was a question."

"I understand. I am fine, thank you."

"Great. Stay comfortable. I am going to ask a very important question. Stay comfortable while you examine the question and give me the truthful answer. Did you kill Carl Powell?"

"No. I killed the werewolf."

"Which werewolf is that?"

"The one that was in possession of Carl."

"Who told you that a werewolf was in possession of Carl?"

"The operator told me."

"Which operator was that?"

"The one immediately preceding you."

"Give me a name."

(Silence).

"Give me a name, Karen."

"I don't remember the name." There was a pause, then one of those subtle shifts. "There is a blockage there."

I was getting help, from God knows where.

"Work around the block."

"We cannot work around the block."

Maybe I did not tell you during the earlier discussion: A hypnotic suggestion (read that, command) can have both a positive and a negative connotation. The subject's own name may be "blocked" by the simple suggestion that he will no longer be able to remember it. Even a numerical concept may be blocked: tell a subject that the number three no longer exists and he cannot perform mathematical computations involving that number. He will not be able, even, to utter the word or to evince a "three" concept.

The most significant thing to me, though, in this particular connection, was the information that "We cannot work around the block." Wherever the help was coming from, it was limited by the physical route. So maybe that "other personality"—whatever or whomever—was in pretty much the same relation to "in-trance Karen" as I was. Interesting idea. There she lay, between us, both of us using her.

"We will let it go for now, then, and maybe we will come back to it later. Stay comfortable."

"I am comfortable."

"Okay. Think about this carefully, now, before you answer. Did you kill your mother and father?"

"I killed my mother."

"Your mother is . . . ?"

"Dead."

"Yes, but give me your mother's name."

"My mother's name was Elena."

"You killed Elena?"

"Yes."

"How did you do that?"

"I blew up the boat."

"But you did not kill your father?"

"No."

"He was on the same boat, wasn't he?"

"No."

"No? TJ was not on the boat?"

"TJ was on the boat. I killed TJ too."

"Let's do this again, Karen. Did you kill your mother and father?"

"I killed Elena and TJ."

"But you did not kill your father?"

"No."

"Who killed him, then?"

"The cancer killed him."

Well, hell, where were we headed? Never mind, I knew exactly where we were headed. And it scared hell out of me.

"What is your father's name, Karen?"

"Joseph Quincy Highland."

"Aren't you confused, dear? Isn't that the name of your grandfather?"

"Yes."

"But it is also the name of your father?"

"Yes."

"Your grandfather is also your father?"

"Yes."

"Package this for me, Karen. We'll come back for it. Okay?"

"Okay."

"What happened to Bruno and Tony?"

"What happened to them?"

"Yes."

"She came for them."

"Who came for them?"

"Elena came for them."

"Why did Elena come for them?"

"They needed her. Elena always took care of Bruno and Tony. When she could."

"Did Elena kill her brothers, Karen?"

"Oh no. I just . . . came . . . to take them . . . home."

Who the hell was I talking to? I was having the devil of a time trying to keep up with it.

"Am I speaking to Karen?"

"Yes." Subtle shift. "With a little help."

"Where is this help coming from?"

"We cannot explain."

"The same as a blockage?"

"The same, yes. Similar."

"Is Karen a murderer?"

"No."

"I don't mean in legal or moral shadings—is she a killer?—has she killed anyone?"

"No."

"Did she blow up a boat?"

"No."

"Did she try to drown Marcia Kalinsky?"

"Not . . . no."

"Did she pick up a rock and bash in the skull of Carl Powell?"

"Her body did."

"But she did not?"

"She did not."

"Have we communicated before? You and me—have we communicated?"

"In a manner, yes."

"Are you Joseph Quincy Highland?"

"I am Karen Highland."

Yes, she was back. But who the hell had I been talking to?

CHAPTER
TWENTY-THREE

Highland

I had the whole thing on tape, using a cassette recorder from Powell's study. Some of my later conclusions were arrived at only after a careful analysis of the material, together with a few leaps of mind, but I had already, at this point, been doing a bit of mental leaping, the constructs of which have been more or less borne out by the final conclusions.

It was not a pretty story, but it was a very human one, perfectly understandable and even worthy of sympathy in its finer movements. I have faithfully transcribed above that portion of the hypnotic session covered thus far, with only a few necessary editorial comments to aid your understanding of what was going on there. The entire session, though, took up that whole Sunday morning, with only a few brief breaks, here and there, to relieve an occasional unbearable tension in the both of us.

I will not burden you with all that detail, much of it given to mental maneuvers and laborious retracings of difficult routes to truth and packaging knowledge as a way around blocks of various types. It is kinder, rather, that I recapitulate and paraphrase the session in a straightforward narrative account, which I have done below, and ask that you simply take my word for it that this is the real story, to the best of my understanding—and about 98.5 percent of it straight out of, or straight through, Karen Highland's mind.

JQ had been a very lonely man, prisoner to his own hermitage, fifty years old and twenty years a widower, when Elena and her brothers came to Highlandville. Elena was about twenty-five, very pretty and vivacious—a real Latin knockout, I guess—well educated, but a bit old-worldly in her moral outlook.

JQ became smitten with Elena, and he proposed marriage shortly after she entered his employ. She declined, but apparently had a fondness for the older man and remained close and supportive until TJ, JQ's son, came home from his latest abortive attempt at college.

I believe, but am not certain, that Terry Kalinsky and TJ were on the same campus at the same time; it is probably not terribly important to the story whether or not they first became acquainted during that period.

TJ and Elena hit it off rather well, rather quickly, and it seems that this bothered JQ—whether from jealousy or whatever. Perhaps it was just because he knew, or had some reason to believe, that any union between the two would be an unhappy one.

He ordered TJ to stay away from Elena.

Elena then threatened to leave.

JQ relented.

TJ and Elena were married in an intimate ceremony at the mansion three months after his return from school.

I get the definite feeling that this marriage was never consummated. Elena began to fade and apparently fell into a deep depression during that first year of marriage.

JQ hired a live-in psychologist to counsel her. She recovered, and there then ensued a renewed camaraderie with JQ. They became intimate and Elena became pregnant.

I do not know what TJ was doing during this period or how he felt about any of it; indeed, TJ appears as little more than a wraith throughout this story—apparently a very solitary and troubled individual, more or less lost in the confines of his own confused reality.

But I do know how JQ felt about it all. He was horrified by Elena's pregnancy, renounced their covert relationship, withdrew from her completely . . . forever.

Even before Karen's birth, Elena's depression returned and deepened. She was in and out of institutions for the rest of her troubled and haunted life, reviving somewhat to some accommodation of her reality only after JQ's death.

Meanwhile, JQ himself showered upon Karen all the love and open affection that he could not or would not bestow upon Karen's mother.

There appears to be no hint that Karen's early life was anything less than happy and healthy. Her troubles began when TJ and Elena perished together on a burning boat, but that was only the beginning of troubles—nothing more remarkable than the trauma that may be experienced by any young girl who awakens one day to find herself alone in the world without family except for two uncles who may not be self-sufficient, themselves, in an open society.

It seems that the real troubles—the hardball kind of troubles—began for Karen only after a certain house physician was added to the staff at Highlandville, and this was some six to seven years following the unfortunate incident with the boat.

The coming of Carl U. Powell—CUP, for short—marked the true beginning of the trouble with Karen.

I have not decided, not even at this writing, if Powell was an evil man, a weak man, or simply an inept and stupid man. I do know, and I know this unequivocally, that he was a terribly destructive influence in Karen's life.

The hypnotherapy was inaugurated within the first few weeks of his arrival at Highlandville. The sessions continued on a twice-weekly basis throughout the following five years.

No wonder(!) that Karen was, by this time, such a remarkably good subject. The conditioning was complete. She could respond to audible triggers, visual triggers, even time triggers—even if these were mixed together in patterns spaced seconds apart. I could touch my left ear and put her in deep trance, touch the right and she is instantly back; wink my left eye to sit her down, the right to start her dancing.

Go to sleep at eight, Karen, and wake up at six. Pee at ten and take a nude dip in the pool at eleven.

He had used her as a guinea pig! As a research subject for his own enlightenment and amusement! The notes, I believe, were for a book he intended to write one day.

Pissed, yeah, I knew a lot of pissed during this investigation. But Powell was not the only culprit, nor necessarily the worst, and apparently he had at last begun to see the damage he had done through his inept tampering with a human soul.

Whether by accidental clumsiness or by design, he had this girl's mind pretty badly scrambled, though, and it was going to take more than one Sunday morning session to put it all back together again in a fully integrated and coherent personality.

And then, of course, there are those "other" entities. I frankly do not know. My jury is still out on this one. I saw things and experienced things that are patently outside the paradigm that guides most of us in our apprehension of reality, but reality is primarily a mental construct, anyway. It does not really matter—or maybe it does, depending on what you are after. If some proof of life after death is what you happen to be after, okay, it matters, and I leave it to you to make your own conclusions.

I was having trouble enough with the instant world, and my troubles were not yet resolved there.

I remembered that Marcia had set up a poolside brunch for twelve-thirty. I called Kalinsky at twelve sharp to make sure that he would be present for that, then I prepared Karen for a final dramatic performance, this latter requiring all of ten minutes working in deep trance with PH triggers.

I figured, what the hell—sauce for the goose, as our old friend Doc Powell had told me some fourteen hours earlier, is also plenty sauce enough for the gander.

We were going to spread some around.

CHAPTER
TWENTY-FOUR
Sauce

Karen looked positively devastating in a white wrap-around skirt over the yellow bikini, sandals, a white carnation in her burgundy hair. She walked with a lively bounce and held my hand as we giggled our way across the patio to join the Kalinskys at brunch.

It was a beautiful autumn day, temperature just right, hardly any smog, sun playing peekaboo among fleecy clouds.

Marcia watched us all the way. As we were seating ourselves at the poolside table, she remarked, a bit archly, "Well, aren't we the young lovers. Karen, honey, you look absolutely smashing."

Karen smiled prettily and replied, "Thanks. I'm feeling great. Better than I've felt in my whole life."

"Not to put a damper on anything," Kalinsky half growled, "but all this gaiety is a little out of keeping with the moment, isn't it?" He gave me a mildly irritated flash of eyes and added, "Or is that the whole idea?"

"It is," I replied. "Ashes to ashes, dust to dust, cry too much and your cheeks will rust."

Karen giggled. Marcia seemed a bit offended, but kept her thoughts to herself.

Kalinsky signaled the waiter and said, sarcastically, "Yeah, that's the spirit."

I showed him a level stare and inquired, "What do you want? Sackcloth and ashes, for God's sake?"

He dropped his gaze, replied, "You're right. Guess I'm just envious. Can't seem to bring myself to that level." He forced a smile, swept it toward Karen, said, "You do look great, honey. I'm glad. Stay that way. We're going to put this whole mess behind us very soon, now."

She said, brightly, "It's already there, TK."

He stared at her for a sober moment, then flashed another smile and said, "That's great."

I scratched my nose with my left hand.

Karen brought a sandaled foot up to rest on the tabletop, fixed Kalinsky with a direct gaze, and asked him, "What's the situation in Addis Ababa?"

He stared at her rather stupidly for a moment before replying, "I guess it's okay."

"What do you mean, it's okay? It'd damn well better be better than okay!"

I could count the confusions in his eyes. He told her, "Well, yes, I think it is. We got out before the damage was done."

I scratched my nose with the other hand.

Karen's foot came down. She leaned toward Marcia and sweetly confided, "I found the yellow bikini. It was right where we left it."

Marcia was looking at it. She said, "So I see. But I saw it on you last night, too, just before dinner."

I scratched the top of my left hand.

Karen scowled at Marcia as she replied, in a harsh tone, "Damned lucky for you that you did, too, but no thanks to your buddy. He fucked my mind, Marcia. He really fucked it over."

Marcia's shocked gaze fled to me, than to Kalinsky, back to Karen. "What?" she managed in a weak voice.

Kalinsky scraped his chair back and growled, "What the hell is going on here?"

I scratched the other hand.

"Shut up!" Karen loudly commanded him. She pushed away a waiter who was trying to transfer food from a serving cart, returned her foot to the table, and told Kalinsky, "On balance, you've done a pretty good job, TK, but you're getting just a little out of hand, don't you think? Don't ever forget where you were and what you were before you came here." She pointed an accusing finger at Marcia and continued, "You too, honey. You're getting to be just a bit too much the whore, don't you think?"

Marcia's chin dropped. She gasped, "Oh my God!"

Kalinsky leaned toward me and whispered in my ear, "What the hell is this, Ash? It's Karen's voice, but it's pure JQ coming through."

I just shook my head and scratched my nose.

Karen stood up and gave the hapless waiter a dazzling smile, said, "Oh, I'm sorry, Charlie—go ahead, please," then did a little pirouette beside Marcia and sang out, "Oh, God, I'm so happy!"

Marcia got to her own feet and embraced Karen a bit awkwardly, gave Kalinsky a baffled look, sat back down, lit a cigarette, looked at me with something approaching anger, said, softly, "Jesus."

I kept it going for another ten minutes or so, totally destroying the brunch while moving Karen alternately across the range of personalities—JQ, Elena, Karen—with rapid-fire changes. A disconcerting array, to say the least—even for me, and I knew the game, though the lines were all spontaneously Karen's, or through Karen, at any rate.

It was destroying Kalinsky too. He had sat unmoving, hunched forward in his chair, staring fixedly at Karen for several minutes.

Marcia, on the other hand, seemed to be paying more attention to me than to Karen—and that was the giveaway—it was what I was looking for. And I had seen enough.

I put a hand on Karen's and said a single word, softly: "Marcia."

Karen turned on her with a fury that surprised even me, crying "Bitch! You rotten bitch! You did that to me!"

Marcia staggered to her feet, wary eyes moving rapidly between Karen and me, finally settling on me as she croaked, "Cute, really cute." She jerked an earlobe and scratched her nose at the same time in a rather discoordinated fashion, then lurched away as Kalinsky came unglued from his chair.

He tried to get a hand on Marcia, but she jerked

away and flung herself across the patio, almost colliding with the serving cart at which Charlie, the waiter, had been trying valiantly, amid all that uproar, to prepare a flambé dish. He had just lit the flame when Marcia brushed him.

I will not say that I absolutely saw a tiny energy pulse hit that dish—but I would almost bet my immortality on it. All I can say for sure is that the whole thing exploded at just that moment, sending Charlie sprawling into the pool, wreathing Marcia and the umbrella above the cart in flames.

I did not hear a sound from Marcia. I doubt that she even knew what hit her. The flaming umbrella immediately collapsed and wrapped itself around her. Kalinsky and I both suffered a few minor burns trying to beat the flames out. We finally pushed the whole blazing pyre into the pool, but it was too late, entirely too late.

I left Kalinsky weeping in the pool, and led a zombied young lady to the Maserati, where then and only then I brought her back to her own true self and took her away from that terribly unhappy place.

Karen's nightmare had ended.

And, though it may sound a bit harsh, some sort of cosmic justice had been served.

EPILOG
Casefile Wrapup

Ashes to ashes, eh?

Well, maybe so.

And maybe not.

You may recall that I reminded you, somewhere during the early going, here, that real life is not a movie script, that things are not always all that cause-and-effect-related in the obvious sense. That was one of the problems I had throughout this case, looking for textures and trying to fit it all, somehow, into a coherent pattern.

But let me assure you that I laid out this case to you exactly as it laid out for me. I kept no secrets, not deliberately—none that matter, anyway—and what you know about the case, right now, is what I knew on that Sunday afternoon when I drove Karen to my place at Malibu.

194

Be assured, also, that I was as bothered then as you may be, now, about various loose ends that were still flapping in the breeze. I tried to pull it all together before it drove me nuts—I talked to Kalinsky by telephone later that same day, and I went down to Marina Del Rey the next day to talk to the forensics people who investigated the boat disaster that killed TJ and Elena Highland. I did some leisurely snooping in Doc Powell's study, though quite a bit later, and I had some rather exhaustive and sometimes interesting interviews with everyone I could find who had worked at the Highland estate over the past quarter century.

Even after all that, though, I still had to leap the mind every now and then to fit a pattern around all the circumstances of this case. I do not know how well I have done that, but at least I finally satisfied myself that I had all the truth worth knowing. I offer that to you here, then, for what it may be worth to you.

First, regarding Marcia: She married young and naive, expecting glamour and excitement in a millionaire's playground, but found instead boredom and lack of purpose in a virtual monastery ruled by an iron-handed, irascible old man who doted on his granddaughter but seemed to despise virtually everyone else. There were no weekend parties in those days, hardly any mingling whatever with the outside world, and it must have been a grim existence for a young woman of high spirit and sociable ways.

Even after JQ died, there seemed to be little relief in that situation. TJ was even more antisocial and reclusive than his father had been, a strange man with strange habits, and his wife was hardly more than an invalid, emerging only now and then for brief periods from her darkened apartment and even then tending to be withdrawn and unapproachable.

A reasonable person may ask, why didn't Marcia simply leave, get out of there, start a new life in a happier environment? Many of us, in that situation, would do exactly that. But consider what you would be giving up. Life at the top, access to billions of dollars, the wildest fantasies imaginable. And only two miserable, pathetic adults standing between you and all that.

Marcia had two active options: to leave, and change her life elsewhere, or to stay, and change her life where she was. I believe that she exercised one of those options. I believe that she went down to Marina Del Rey one sunny morning and tampered with the gas tank on TJ's boat.

After that, she became lady of the house. She opened it up, brought some life inside, and I believe that she actually tried to become a mother figure to Karen. Perhaps she even convinced herself that she had performed a noble service for the teenager, rescuing her from the gloomy and depressing influence of her parents and opening the world to her. There is evidence to suggest this.

It is a sad and tragic web that we weave, though, once we cross the line into nefarious plots and stealthy deceits. It is as though somehow the very soul becomes imprinted with these crimes, the personality changes, and the next time out is always a shade easier.

Marcia got into a lot of dumb shit across those years. Among other things, she had an affair with the operations manager and, with him, succeeded in diverting several hundred thousand dollars to a Hong Kong bank account. This occurred before Karen's twentieth birthday, but did not come out until after Marcia's death. There were various other thieveries, as well, but none quite so immaculate and ambitious as the opportunity that presented itself via Carl Powell and his hypnotic tampering with the heiress to billions.

This was to be her grand slam—and, again, maybe she told herself that no one would even miss a few lousy million out of all those riches. Marcia had been earning ten thousand a year when she met and married Terry Kalinsky. TK, developing his business mind at JQ's shoulder, so to speak, made her sign a premarital agreement limiting her community property share of joint income to that same ten grand per year plus a "raise" of one percent annually. She'd married young, remember, and she may have later reflected bitterly on that financial state of affairs—especially when it became apparent that her husband was becoming a multimillionaire in his own right.

At any rate, Marcia—with the help of her new lover, Carl Powell, found a way to get even, a way that was just too slick to pass up.

TK found all this a bit hard to swallow. If you believe the guy, and I do, his wife never once complained to him about the financial arrangements.

"If she had," he said miserably, "I would have torn up the damned premarital agreement and burned it in a candlelight and wine ceremony. Hell, I just never thought about it. I doubt that it could have withstood a legal challenge, anyway, especially after all these years."

You hear a lot about the value of good communications between husband and wife. So there you go . . . a case in point. TK had really, deeply, been in love with his wife all those years. He just had a hard time showing it.

Marcia's remains were cremated on Monday, completing the grim task that had begun beside the pool on Sunday. There was a brief service at a Beverly Hills chapel on Tuesday, which Karen and I both attended, and we had coffee with TK after the service at a private club on Wilshire. He was distraught. His eyes watered a lot and his lower lip quivered occasionally as he told us about Marcia's "indiscretions."

It was during this conversation that I learned about the episode with the bank in Hong Kong. But there was more, quite a bit more, and the revelations were being directed primarily at Karen—perhaps as an apology, but also almost as a confessional in which TK was assuming most of the blame for all that had gone wrong.

"I knew she was getting screwed up. I just didn't know how bad it had become. And I blame myself for not being sensitive to her concerns." He placed a hand on Karen's and tried but failed to maintain eye contact with her as he continued. "I can't believe that she really meant to harm you, honey. But I have found a number of postdated documents—do you remember signing . . . ?"

Karen shook her head in a vague response. "Documents? I don't . . . remember. . . . "

He sighed. "Well, you made her a very rich woman, or she would have been next Saturday." He glanced at me. "All perfectly legal, on the surface. Drawn up by a law firm in Westwood. Could Karen have been made to do something like that while in one of those trances?"

I said, "Sure. She would stand by them, too, if—"

Karen's eye flashed and she slapped a palm against her forehead as she cried, "Oh, those documents. Of course I remember. No, those are okay, they are okay, I want them to stand just as they are."

TK was giving her another of those flabbergasted gazes. I caught his eye and showed him a small jerk of the head as I quietly commented, "We will remove all this debris. Don't worry about it."

Karen asked, "What debris?"

I explained, "Marcia and Carl were manipulating you, Karen, using hypnosis. It will take a while, but we will comb through all the buried PH's and dispose of them."

She seemed confused, almost agitated.

I told TK, "It's okay, normal response. A PH takes the form of a compulsion. We just have to find them all and neutralize them."

He shot Karen an uncomfortable look as he growled, "Well, I guess that answered my question."

If things had proceeded apace, Karen would not only have stood by those documents but would have come up with all manner of rationalizations to explain the action. In that latter connection, remember the incident in her bedroom when I had her close out the coming storm.

But things did not proceed apace. They started going to hell in a basket, maybe because Carl had begun to realize what havoc he had wrought in Karen's personality—maybe simply because Carl became afraid of Marcia or afraid of Marcia's husband; you decide. I do know that Carl was the moving factor in bringing Karen to my attention.

Karen had never been to Zodiac. Carl had. I found a copy of my treatise on cosmic sex in his stuff. I do not know for sure exactly what he had in mind for me, but I suspect that he may have been genuinely looking for help in his dilemma. I do know, also, that Carl went to TK several days before I joined the play and made his peace, there, apologizing for the affair with Marcia and assuring TK that he was leaving Highlandville alone—this, after the confrontation between the two reported to me by the bartender, Ramirez.

I believe that my entrance onto the scene scared the pee out of Marcia. I have already suggested, earlier, that she was a believer in psychic power and may have been prepared to believe that I could "read" her mind. The lady had a lot to hide.

I believe that she "operated" Karen into the nude scene at poolside that Saturday afternoon. Why? Hell, I don't know why. I don't read minds. Maybe she thought it would scare me away, or lead me astray—who knows?—or maybe it was just a cutesy trick to liven up a boring afternoon. Maybe it was just an extension of the movement begun by Powell. He "sent" Karen to me, in the first place, with a story patently designed to intrigue and—he thought, I'm sure—guarantee my attention and involvement with Karen.

Maybe Marcia operated Karen into nothing but the nude scene; the rest, conceivably—the shocking announcement that I was there to provide her with orgasms—a carryover from another PH planted by Powell earlier, working as a rationalization. Remember that in a PH the operator does not have to write the script; a staging prompt is quite sufficient. The subject, in carrying out the prompt, will write his own script.

It seems likely, especially now with the benefit of some cool aftersight, that Marcia—as of the moment when I arrived on the scene—knew, or at least suspected, that something had changed in her relationship with Carl Powell. I doubt that she would have wanted me there, especially during this final countdown of days before her grand slam. She was already disturbed and/or uneasy before I made the scene. My arrival deepened her anxiety.

I asked TK about that, during that same conversation over coffee following Marcia's funeral service. His eyes watered as he thoughtfully replied, "I'm sure that's true, Ash. I knew about her affair with Carl, of course. I even discussed it with Carl. A couple of times. Never with her, though. Hell . . . I understood. I just wanted to be sure that he didn't leave scars on her. And I flat put my foot down when he told me that he was taking Marcia to Europe with him. I mean, how did I know he wouldn't get tired of it and dump her somewhere? What the hell? Yes, I put my foot down. Not to Marcia. To Carl. He fussed back, made some dumb threats. But then I guess after he had a chance to think it over he decided he didn't want her that bad, after all. I doubt that he told her about that, though. Not his style. He would have just slipped away in the night, left her holding her packed bags and nowhere to go. But Marcia was not a dummy. She probably knew. And, yes, you scared hell out of her. I could read that. She didn't know anything about you until you showed up at the house. She was in a tizzy, I could tell."

And then one of those nontextual events occurred to really tizzy things. Or maybe it was purely contextual, if you choose to accept otherworldly influences. Marcia nearly drowned. She saw Karen standing there in the shadows at poolside, and she was believer enough to ascribe some psychic phenomenon to the event.

So—was Karen "out of control"? Or was someone "operating" on Marcia, through Karen? We have to read "someone" as Carl Powell, of course. And we can now view the near-drowning as a crucial moment for Marcia and as the catalyst that moved this drama into rapid climax.

TK remembers that when Karen visited Marcia after dinner, that Saturday night, he left the two women alone briefly at Marcia's request for a glass of water. When he returned with the water, their heads were together in what seemed at the time an intimate conversation. Moments later, Marcia threw the water at Karen and emotionally accused her.

Apparently that was the "trigger." From that moment, Karen was acting out a posthypnotic suggestion under hallucinatory influences.

Carl Powell knew exactly where to look for Karen—perhaps he checked with Marcia first?—on a small meadow within a canyon where wild flowers grow, Karen's favorite retreat—a place, now, in the imposed nightmarish shadows of Karen's delusions, where werewolves and demons roamed the night. Maybe the doc had good reasons for wanting to get there first, and alone—suspecting what Marcia had done—or maybe he was just plain scared out of his skull and wondering if his "experiment" had, indeed, gone out of control.

I have not decided why Marcia had earlier tried to plant a suspicion of Kalinsky in my mind, unless it was just another try at scaring me off.

The little showdown over brunch was a regrettable but necessary affair. I was still reaching for answers, not really sure which way the thing was going to go. I had to find the "operator." You may recall that I had found the code by comparing doodles—Kalinsky's and Powell's—which definitely had me tilted toward TK as the villain, and I have to admit that I went into that little act prepared to react accordingly, the Walther PPK still tucked into the waistband of my shorts.

TK told me, with obvious embarrassment, "Sure, I knew he was using hypnosis. And I knew that he had this trick word, but, shit, I swear to you I had never seen the thing working, not to my knowledge at the time, for damned sure."

He shivered, remembering. "Scares hell out of me, to tell the truth. I couldn't do that. It's funny, though—I knew, I mean I was sure that you were doing something, but I couldn't figure out what it was. Besides, I was too much into what was happening to wonder a lot about how. I never heard you say 'Elena Magdalena.' "

Karen immediately said, "Yes, I understand."

TK gawked at her and whispered, "Oh shit!"

I chuckled as I told him, "We'll get rid of that, too, at the proper time. Tell her to wake up."

He was still whispering: "You tell her."

I said, "Can't. You're the operator. She can't even hear me until you tell her that she may."

TK whispered to her, "Listen to Ash, honey. Do what he says."

Karen turned to me and said, "Yes, I understand."

I said, "Wake up, Karen."

She showed a beautiful smile and asked, still in the earlier conversation, "Exactly what were we doing?"

TK sighed and passed a hand over his eyes and rested it on the bridge of his nose, inspecting his lovely ward with an intent stare. He was clean, I was sure of that. Too bad I couldn't have been that sure at noon on Sunday.

What threw me off was an erroneous leap of mind. TK wanted the operator, yes, but because he saw it as a way to protect Karen, as a control feature. I do believe that Powell sincerely wrestled with his conscience over that idea, as rightly he should have. We have seen the damage that may be done by inept handling of that kind of power.

I believe, also, but not with any particular conviction, that Powell did not deliberately hand over to Marcia the keys to Karen's mind. Anyway, I prefer to think that way. Give the dead the benefit of any doubt—Marcia easily could have wormed her way into that situation without Powell's knowledge, or at least without his connivance.

As for Powell threatening Kalinsky, during the argument overheard by the bartender, Ramirez, to the effect that Powell had incriminating evidence on Kalinsky—I simply have to discount it as heated blustering on Powell's part, maybe as desperate blustering by a very frightened man who might well have entertained unfounded suspicions. My ongoing investigation found no hint whatever that Terry Kalinsky had behaved irresponsibly or criminally in any way.

There is a final, fat question concerning Marcia. Why, after all that scheming toward her grand slam, did she then turn about during the final countdown of days to propel Karen into an action that would most certainly postpone, maybe forever, the turnover of the estate to Karen?

Sigh. Another noncontextual event? Maybe. Or maybe Marcia just wasn't smart enough—or stable enough, within herself—to think through the cause-and-effect logic of that. Maybe she simply panicked and reacted blindly to what she perceived as an attack on her by her erstwhile lover, Carl Powell—a woman scorned in the worst possible way—and she was simply playing tit for tat. That is the way I am reading it, for the record, if only because that reading provides context of a sort—a context within a context, if you will.

She was smart enough, though—after the fact, anyway—to make sure that I knew that she was planning to run away with the victim of her "murder by remote control."

That about covers the heavy stuff.

There are a few side issues still at large, though. Such as the Valensa brothers. I have more or less accepted their deaths as by natural causes, the same in both cases. The rare genetic defect that hampered their full expression of life also contained, I am told, some sort of built-in disconnect that operates after a given number of cell divisions—a sort of built-in biological time clock that brings death in midlife. Both died at the age of forty-six. In this connection, there is something eerie yet also quite poignant in Karen's in-trance inference that Elena knew the appointed time and had "come for them." But you figure it out for yourself.

I guess I will always wonder, though, about my own doctor, my drinking buddy who came to my place in Malibu that Friday night to check on Karen. Guy was only about forty, in apparent good health, but dropped dead with a coronary attack during a party at a neighbor's house. I hate nontextual complications when working in a logic pattern, but there you go—those things do happen—real life ain't a movie.

As for TK, I have to tell you that we have become friends, if not exactly drinking buddies. He's a bit too rigid for my buddying tastes, but he really is a pretty good guy. He brokered out at a hundred mil as his share of Highlandville—can you believe that?—but the record shows that he had appreciated the estate four times that during his eleven years at the helm, so what the hell. Despite his own independent status as a very rich man, he remains on with Karen as of this writing, supposedly until she gets her feet firmly onto ground, but I think the guy will die there.

All the intrigue on that Saturday night with the legal eagles and the conservancy trick was really a brilliant stroke, and I have to give the guy credit. He had been greatly concerned about Karen's mental health, of course, especially considering the family history—which is why he brought Powell on board, in the first place—then the stuff Powell started feeding him was enough to cinch a growing panic.

Karen had indeed been showing visible symptoms of all the hardball ailments described by Powell—but, of course, and I believe this with all my heart and mind, all but about one percent of those hardball ailments had been engineered by Powell in his clumsy invasions of her person. It is all to TK's credit, though, that he had a contingency plan all set up to forestall any emergency situation and to give his charge all possible protection under the law. She still enjoys that protection, by the way, and we have a sympathetic judge who has been fully clued-in to all the happenings out there; Karen is going to be okay in the legal department, and she will be certified sane and ready to accept all of life's responsibilities most any day now.

As for Karen, herself, I do not mind saying that this is one of the loveliest and most lovable women I have ever known. She was not half bad with all her problems; now that she is blossoming out into her true self, the girl is simply devastating. There was no Electra complex there, by the way, and certainly no latent nymphomania, not unless there is something essentially unhealthy about a good, strong sex drive.

In that particular connection, and no pun intended, it was a remotely controlled Karen who went seeking a sexual surrogate, of course, so I will forever be thankful that I did not fall in with that error. You may recall—I may have mentioned, earlier—that I never felt "right" in that situation. I have learned, since, that Karen had not experienced orgasms because she had never experienced the sexual embrace. She thought about it a lot, sure, anyone will, anyone who has a normal drive, and it was probably this sort of fantasy-play shadowy stuff that Powell seized upon, unable himself to distinguish reality-memories from fantasy-memories.

Anyway, let me assure you that Karen is whole and healthy in matters of sex as well as all the others. It would not be proper to mention this, here, except that—as you must have already surmised—I have changed all the names here for reasons of privacy and confidentiality. Karen and I have had several long, philosophical discussions on the subject of "cosmic sex"—and, of course, you will remember that we had one of those soul-bonding experiences early in our relationship. Relationship, yeah, we have one of those. I think we are about ready, in fact, to give cosmic sex a whirl—and, frankly, I can hardly wait to try my own theories.

I guess there is a final item awaiting disposal. JQ. A hell of a guy, I think, and I wish I'd known him in the flesh. Is he actually Karen's biological father? Hell, I don't know. Not sure enough, anyway, to integrate any of that into Karen's new personality. For the purposes of this particular lifetime, how could it possibly matter, anyway, at this stage of things?

Karen knows that she has been greatly loved and cherished, and who can ask for more than that?

What prompted the last-minute change of heart concerning his estate? I simply cannot say. The mere existence of that document, though of no legal significance whatever, has scarred forever the sensitivities of Terry Kalinsky. That is about the only effect I can find. And I have pointed out to TK that any number of emotions could have been working at that dying and tortured mind, none of which would have to have roots in a distrust of Kalinsky, himself.

JQ could have been worried about Elena. Maybe, and this is a strong possibility, he could have seen something in the maturing Marcia Kalinsky that set his teeth on edge and turned his thoughts to countermeasures. Or, possibly, he was worried that his own son would assert himself as a man, upon the father's death, and move bitterly against a patently unfair division of the estate; given that situation, all manner of scandalous dirt could have titillated the nation for years.

See—it's not a script, it's real life.

And real life is never all that certain.

Unless, of couse . . . well, if you take the whole bag . . . I mean, what is life, anyway—where does it begin and where does it end, really, or does it ever do either one? What the hell is really going on here, in this place only perceptible by, and probably largely created by our sensory apparatus?—what does it all mean?—where are we all headed?

I don't have the answer to any of that, mind you.

But, uh, I have a new drinking buddy.

I do all the drinking, but I somehow get the feeling that he smacks what passes for lips in some other reality and enjoys the process as much as I do.

And maybe, just maybe, one day he will drop another book at my feet—and who knows what answers I may come up with, then.

Okay. That's about it. Got to go, now. Have a date with Karen. We're driving up to Zodiac for the weekend. In pursuit of truth. Yeah. The cosmic truth.

'Til later . . . see you around.

Mystery . . . Intrigue
. . . Suspense

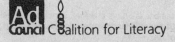